I0573261

Credits

<table>
<tr><td>

Author
John M. Stater

Developers
Bill Webb

Producer
Bill Webb of Necromancer Games

Editor
Bill Webb of Necromancer Games

Layout and Production
Charles A. Wright

Front Cover Art
MKUltra Studios

</td><td>

Interior Art
Rowena Aitken

Cartography
Robert Altbauer

Playtesters
Frog God Games Staff

Special Thanks
Bill Webb would like to thank Bob Bledsaw and Bill Owen for inventing the original hex crawl — the standard in wilderness adventure and a lifetime of fun.

</td></tr>
</table>

©2011 Bill Webb, John Stater, Frog God Games. All rights reserved. Reproduction without the written permission of the publisher is expressly forbidden. Frog God Games and the Frog God Games logo and Splinters of Faith are trademarks of Frog God Games. All rights reserved. All characters, names, places, items, art and text herein are copyrighted by Frog God Games, Inc. The mention of or reference to any company or product in these pages is not a challenge to the trademark or copyright concerned.

Table of Contents

Hex Crawl Chronicles

— The Winter Woods —

By John M. Stater

The Winter Woods are situated in the northern climes where the snow falls from late Autumn to early Spring. The map can be roughly divided into five geographical regions. The extreme west is a land of thickly wooded canyons, mesas and buttes divided by rushing streams that flow into the Great River, visible in the southwest corner of the map. The north central portion of the map is a rolling prairie of tall grasses, wildflowers, leaping gazelles, browsing wisent and mammoth and prowling smilodons. The prairie and canyon lands are bordered on the east by a land of forested hills, gentle compared to the western lands, and very fertile. The extreme east of the map contains what the native folk call the "Black Water", a vast sea of viscous, black water that gives off an acrid smell and is said to harbor things better left unseen. The shores of the Black Water are a moor of black, spongy ground and perverse fungal growths, some growing as tall as trees. The natives of the Winter Woods believe they know what lies beyond the Black Water, but are hesitant ever to speak of it lest "they" prick up their ears and take an interest in the teller of tales.

The native Hivernians will tell you that the land is now as it has always been, a battlefield between the forces of Spring and the forces of Winter. The Black Water and the lands that border it have always been a gateway to the Land of the Dead, and always best avoided. The Hivernians have always had to scrape and fight to survive in the Winter Woods, coping with the Queen of the Winter Wind when she roams the land, rejoicing when she does not. The colonizing Northmen are a bother, but really just one more problem to be overcome.

The Northmen came to the Winter Wood just a couple generations ago, following Prince Polominen in his quest to write a brilliant new chapter in the history of his father's glorious empire. Many followed – adventurers, traders, tenant farmers seeking to become yeomen in their own right. The Northmen poured into the Winter Woods, colonizing the southern portions, pushing the Hivernians into the north and ignoring their warnings that their doom was rapidly approaching. In time, the Hivernians were proved right, as the capital city of the Northmen was overcome by the Black Water, its people reduced to madness. With the fall of the Northmen's Empire to the south and east, the remaining colonists find themselves in a very serious predicament – one that requires great heroes or offers wondrous opportunities for base villains. Enter, the player characters …

The Winter Woods is a hex-crawl, referring to the hex-shaped units that divide the map. Just as dungeon adventures take place on a gridded map, wilderness adventures can be conducted on a hex map, allowing players the freedom to decide where their characters roam and giving them the thrill of discovering the many places and people that have been placed on the map. This map represents a large area filled with numerous places to discover and explore, and can be used as a campaign area in its own right, or dropped into an existing campaign. Referees can place adventures they have purchased or devised on their own into empty hexes on the map.

Adventures in the Wilderness

The hexes on this map are 6 miles wide from one side to the other. In open country, adventurers should be able to see from one side of the hex to another. In wooded hexes, vision is much more restricted. Random encounters with monsters should be diced for each day and each night, with encounters occurring on the roll of 1-2 on 1d6. The exact monster (or monsters) encountered depends on the terrain through which the adventurers are traveling. Unlike dungeons, in which the monsters on the upper levels are usually less powerful than the monsters on deeper levels, wilderness encounters are quite variable in their challenge, and low level characters face death every time they step out of the confines of civilization. Well traveled adventurers will discover, however, that settled lands are not as dangerous as the rugged wilderness.

Roll	Black Water (8)	Grasslands (5)	Moors (6)	Wooded Hills (4)
1	Aboleth (1d8)	Ankheg (1d8)	Alligator, Giant (2d6)	Boar, Wild (2d6)
2	Black Ark (1)	Badger, Giant (2d6)	Berserker (2d6+10)	Berserker (2d6+6)
3	Ghoul (2d6+6)	Berserker (2d6+6)	Centipede, Giant Man-Sized (2d6+6)	Gnoll (2d6+6)
4	Locathah (3d6+6)	Blink Dog (2d8)	Dryad (2d6+6)	Goblin (3d6+6)
5	Nixie (3d6+6)	Eagle, Giant (2d6)	Frog, Giant (2d8)	Owlbear (1d8)
6	Sea Serpent (1)	Goblin (3d6+6)	Gnoll (2d6+10)	Patrol (see below)
7	Troll (2d6)	Hobgoblin (3d6+6)	Goblin (3d6+6)	Skunk, Giant (1d8)
8	Zombie (3d6+6)	Mastodon (1d4)	Mushroom Man (2d6)	Wendigo (2d6)
9	—	Patrol (see below)	Spider, Giant Man-Sized (2d6)	Werebear (1d6)
10	—	Smilodon (1d6)	Violet Fungi (2d6+6)	Werewolf (1d8)
11	—	Werewolf (2d6)	Will-o-the-Wisp (1d6)	Winter Wolf (1d8)
12	—	Worg (2d6)	Zombie (2d6+6)	Worg (2d6)

Note: The ghouls, ogres and trolls of the Black Water are all aquatic versions of the normal creatures, with webbed fingers and toes and the ability to swim at their normal movement rate and breathe water (although ghouls, being undead, needn't breathe at all). Zombies are humanoids who have died at sea or galley slaves from the black arks that have somehow fallen overboard. The dryads of the moors and fungal forests inhabit giant mushrooms instead of trees, and are slightly more madcap. Otherwise, they use the normal stats for a dryad.

Black Arks

The black arks are tall galleys with three levels of oars but lacking sails. As one might imagine, they are constructed from a black wood, sealed with tar and equipped with rams of black-bronze. The arks are rowed by untiring zombies and crewed by mysterious men from beyond the Black Water. These men are tall and hunched. They wear layers of gauzy black robes, veils and turbans and take great pains to keep their hands hidden. Beyonders always carry curved blades at their sides. Some say that they are zombies, ghouls or demons beneath their robes, others that they are merely shriveled, hideous humans. Most black arks carry two or three of the men, nicknamed Beyonders, and a complement of thirty skeleton warriors armed with spears and longbows. Each Beyonder can cast cleric spells as clerics of level 1st to 6th (roll 1d6) and magic-users of level 1st to 4th (roll 1d4).

Beyonder: HD 4d6; AC 7 [12]; Atk 1 weapon (1d6+1); Move 9; Save 13 (9 vs. poison and magic); CL/XP 5/240 or 6/400; Special: Cast cleric and magic-user spells.

Men

As mentioned above, there are two societies of men in the Valley, the colonizing Northmen who have been cut off from their homeland, and the native Hivernians.

The **Northmen** have ebony or chocolate skin and wavy hair of brown or black, often worn long. Northmen tend to be stout and plump, and they are known for their baggy trousers and long tunics. They favor axes and curved knives and usually wear chainmail or platemail in battle. The Northmen of the Winter Woods are pioneers, and notably more fit and rugged than their effete counterparts back home.

Berserkers are usually descendants of the Northmen who settled the City of Madness, wandering the land, dazed and paranoid. These men and women are sometimes armed with clubs or even axes, but just as often fight with tooth and nail. They are shabbily dressed, rarely armored, and really only constitute a threat because of their bloodlust.

The **Hivernians** have jaundiced, sallow skin and hair that ranges from dark carnelian to fiery orange. Their eyes are icy blue. Hivernians are short and wiry, with long arms, fingers and toes, pug noses, long teeth and heavy jaws. They wear animal skins and long hoods decorated with bones and teeth. They carry spears and short bows and wear the equivalent of leather armor. Their leaders are skilled in stalking and hunting. Hivernians worship the elk-antlered, doe eyed goddess Yhoundeh.

Patrols are from the town of Yaryg or a nearby stronghold. Each patrol contains 1d6+6 men-at-arms mounted on horses, wearing ring mail and carrying shield, lance, long sword and light crossbow. Each patrol is led by a sergeant wearing chainmail, but otherwise armed as his men.

Man-At-Arms: HD 1; AC 5 [14]; Atk 1 weapon (1d8); Move 9 (18 on horseback); Save 17; CL/XP 1/15; Special: None.

Sergeant: HD 3; AC 3 [16]; Atk 1 weapon (1d8); Move 9 (18 on horseback); Save 14; CL/XP 3/60; Special: None.

Rumors

When adventurers are seeking information or rumors in a settlement or from the lord of a castle, you can roll a random rumor from the table below. Each rumor is either True ("T") or False ("F") and the hex number associated with the rumor is given in brackets.

Roll	Rumor	Roll	Rumor
1	Don't mess about with Povis' gardens – they're protected by demons! (T) Hex 0225	11	The maze maiden has knowledge of the Winter Queen (F) Hex 1513
2	The north country is the domain of a demonic queen (T) Hex 0402	12	Mushroom men are rarely violent if presented with a gift of dung (F) Hex 2116
3	The hills hold a wondrous spring that cures all ills (F) Hex 0425	13	The goblins are preparing for war! (T) Hex 2306
4	Beotem conjures demons in his forge and traps them in his weapons (F) Hex 0612	14	Fie on this Winter Queen nonsense – Exfreza is who you really have to watch (F) Hex 2416
5	The dragon of the wood is friendlier than most of his kind (T) Hex 0701	15	Sibevi would pay handsomely for the undoing of her sister Exfreza (F) Hex 2716
6	The woods are full of werewolves these days – nobody can be trusted (T)	16	There is a tomb of the gods hidden in the hills (T) Hex 3210
7	The Spider Eater is a vampire (F) Hex 0906	17	So help me, there are purple dwarves living in the moors, and they're wicked! (T) Hex 3510
8	The Winter Queen hides in a vale of shadows (F) Hex 1115	18	The Vicar is not to be trusted (F) Hex 0116
9	Hill giants dig pits around their homes, so beware (T) Hex 1203	19	Cwelfalys is no friend of Northmen (T) Hex 0814
10	Yelllow grass means death – turn back! (T) Hex 1503	20	The Queen of the Winter Wind's soul inhabits a secret labyrinth in the woods. (?) Hex 1513

Encounter Key

0108.

Xydry is a small village of Hivernian hunters. The village consists of a circular rampart of packed earth about 10-feet in height. Stone huts are built against this rampart, with small cellars dug into the earth and holding smoked meats, berries and other foodstuffs gathered by the village women. In the center of the village there is a wide pit into which captives are thrown to be devoured by a grizzled old cave bear or a pack of fierce wolves. The villagers are divided into two clans, cave bear and wolf. The clans despise one another, and are only held together by a marriage alliance between their leaders, the great hunter Logre and the witch woman Sulic. The fighting pit is constructed over a subterranean chamber that can be entered via the aforementioned cellars. This low-ceilinged chamber holds a small idol carved from a large chunk of rock crystal (worth 500 gp). The idol depicts the Devourer, the savage god of winter. The Devourer appears as a gaunt, almost skeletal figure with an oversized head and eyes as large as saucers. It has a wide grin and long fingers, and sits in a fetal position on the pelt of a winter wolf (worth 1,000 gp). The idol is surrounded by clay pots filled with offerings of offal and teeth.

Logre of the Wolf Clan, Fighter Lvl 3: HP 16; AC 6 [13]; Atk 1 weapon (1d6+1); Move 12; Save 12; CL/XP 3/60; Special: None. Leather armor, leather buckler, spear, short bow. A layer of fat over powerful muscles, bears many scars, unhappy with his wife and has a mischievous streak.

Sulic of the Cavebear Clan, Cleric Lvl 5: HP 18; AC 6 [13]; Atk 1 weapon (1d4); Move 12; Save 11 (9 vs. paralysis and poison); CL/XP 6/400; Special: Cleric spells (2nd), turn undead. Leather armor, club of white wood studded with pieces of quartz. Shy and eccentric in manner, she is lean and has a long, morose face.

0111.

A small party became lost here last winter and turned to cannibalism to survive. Now wendigos, they haunt the area and are encountered on a roll of 1-5 on 1d6. Before their possession by the feral spirits of the forest, they were a cleric, two dwarves, a female magic-user and two fighting-men.

Wendigo: HD 4; AC 4 [15]; Atk 1 bite (1d6); Move 15; Save 13; CL/XP 4/120; Special: Immune to cold, only killed by silver or magic weapons – otherwise regenerate 2 hp per turn after "death".

0116.

Trifforth is a large village of Northmen on the banks of the Great River. The villagers primarily herd sheep and keep prairie chickens and geese. The village is situated in the bottom of a wide canyon with walls that range from 200 to 300 tall. A winding stair has been carved in the southern wall of the canyon to allow access to a high beacon tower of stone manned by the guardsmen of the village. The village proper consists of hundreds of thatched houses huddled around a large, stone citadel ruled by a man called "The Vicar", a fiery cleric who preaches a religion of thrift, discipline and self-denial. He is assisted by four acolytes and all wear long hauberks of chainmail and carry shields emblazoned with a large eye surrounded by a fiery aura. The women of the village are known for their knitwork, and the village has many shepherds knowledgable about the surrounded wooded hills and maybe willing to work as guides. The guides work cheap, but their constant singing of hymns often drives others to distraction (surprised on 1-2 on 1d6).

Treasure: 690 sp, 80 gp.

The Vicar, Cleric Lvl 5: HP 21; AC 3 [16]; Atk 1 weapon (1d8); Move 9; Save 11 (9 vs. paralysis and poison); CL/XP 6/400; Special: Cleric spells (2nd), turn undead. Chainmail, shield, mace, holy symbol carved from polished coral (worth 600 gp, +1 to turn wraiths). Stubborn and severe, tall with a bland face and grey-green eyes.

Acolytes, Clerics Lvl 1: HD 1d6+1; AC 3 [16]; Atk 1 weapon (1d8); Move 9; Save 15 (13 vs. paralysis and poison); CL/XP 1/15; Special: Turn undead. Chainmail, shield, mace.

0118.

This river canyon is home to a tribe of pitch black ogres with flat faces, narrow, yellow eyes and great tusks that nearly curl up to their bald scalps. These ogres are more intelligent than the norm and strangely resistant to magic. They are commanded by an ogre mage call Zimblak, who keeps a kennel of shadow mastiffs to guard the tunnels of his subterranean fortress. The halls of Zimblak's fortress are inhabited by wall-crawling red rats, goblin guardians in armor made of bronze coins and carrying sticky nets and barbed whips, sparkling cider oozes and wandering clouds that induce feelings of terror, rage and despair. At the heart of Zimblak's fortress lies an ancient dwarf tomb that the ogre mage has never managed to penetrate.

Zimblak: HD 5+4 (30 hp); AC 4 [15]; Atk 1 weapon (1d12); Move 12 (F18); Save 12; CL/XP 7/600; Special: Magic use.

0202.

This territory is claimed by a pack of fifteen winter wolves. The wolves are led by a massive alpha male that the goblins proclaim the "Wolf God". From their ranks are selected a few steeds for the goblin chieftains of the Winter Woods. The wolves have a den in an expansive cave, the rear of which is covered in ice. It is in this ice that the wolves freeze extra provender (e.g. victims) and treasure. Currently they have three or four frozen bodies (a cleric, two peasants and a rotund halfling with a surprised look on his fat face) as well as 1,400 gp and a silver idol of a stately woman with amber eyes and two massive tusks jutting up from her lower jaw. The tusks are ivory and taken from a giant boar. The idol is worth 10,000 gp and weighs about 200 pounds.

Winter Wolf: HD 5; AC 5 [14]; Atk 1 bite (1d6+1); Move 18; Save 12; CL/XP 6/400; Special: Breathe frost (range 10-ft, 4d6 damage, once per turn).

Wolf God: HD 7 (40 hp); AC 5 [14]; Atk 1 bite (1d8+1); Move 18; Save 9; CL/XP 8/800; Special: Breathe frost.

0205.

A copse of trees near the river are bloated and black. They drip red sap the looks and smells like blood and acts as a sleep poison when used to coat weapons. Goblin archers make use of this poison and patrols of 1d6+6 goblins are encountered here on a roll of 1-3 on 1d6.

Goblins: HD 1d6; AC 6 [13]; Atk 1 weapon (1d6); Move 9; Save 18; CL/XP B/10; Special: -1 to hit in sunlight. Leather armor, shields, short swords, short bows.

0212.

Three tall, bent pine trees support the webbing of an immense spider. The spider is intelligent and has at its command thousands of normal spiders. These spiders serve as its spies, dispersing into the outer region and bringing back rumors and stories. The giant spider is something of a sage and it can cast divination spells as a 7th level magic-user. Winning its confidence often requires the performance of tasks most folk would blanche at even considering, for the spider has a grisly taste for children. At any given time, it can throw up to 3 spider swarms against its foes.

Giant Spider: HD 7 (24 hp); AC 6 [13]; Atk 1 bite (1d8 + poison); Move 18; Save 9; CL/XP 9/1100; Special: Spells (4th, divinations only), poison (save or die).

Spider Swarm: HD 2; AC 7 [12]; Atk 1 swarm (1 + poison); Move 18; Save 16; CL/XP 3/60; Special: Poison (-1 to all d20 rolls, cumulative with each failed saving throw), covers a 10-ft x 10-ft area, minimum damage from non-bludgeoning or area effect attacks.

0225.

An enterprising trader named Povis has turned the skeleton of a giant pteranodon into a weird roadhouse. The roadhouse is well known to travelers from the Valley of the Hawk to the southwest, and it is not uncommon for a caravan to be camped out around the building. The roadhouse consists of great tarpons of leather covered with oilcloth stretched over the bones of the great beast. A flap grants access to the house proper, which consists of a sunken chamber lined with golden brown bricks and containing a long table and benches and four smaller tables. In one corner of the room there are three kegs fitted into the stone wall and the landlord, Povis, pouring sparkling ales, frothy beers and crisp wines into mugs and goblets. A short stone staircase leads to an underground passageway with three doors – one to a kitchen (the chimney can be seen poking out of the ground when

Black Water
Cold River
West River
East River
Serpent's Tongue
Sable River
Great River

folk first view the strange house) and the other two to dormitories. The kitchen has doors leading to a root cellar and sleeping quarters for Povis, his wife Floris, his two children Monk and Gloris, and their servants – a wench named Janua and a groom called Pickle. The Dead Dragon Inn has no private rooms, but Povis does keep a locked iron strongbox in his room for storing valuables. The Dead Dragon's kitchen serves quite a lot of salt pork, often in a stew with broad beans and potatoes. Swine are herded in the surrounding woods and the staff tends a large medicinal and kitchen garden surrounded by a low, stone wall. Besides traveling merchants, the inn attracts lumberjacks (often drunk and rowdy), rangers and other adventurers. Povis is a retired magic-user who still retains a knack for enchanting gourds with ghostly lights (he keeps them around his establishment in the dark days of fall and winter). He has also animated a jack-o'-lantern headed scarecrow to protect his garden from intruders.

Povis, Magic-User Lvl 6: HP 19; AC 9 [10]; Atk 1 dagger (1d4); Move 12; Save 10 (8 vs. spells); CL/XP 7/600; Special: Spells (3rd). Peasant's clothes, leather vest, white oak wand, silver dagger. A Northman with white hair, green eyes and a fat, unexpressive face. He enjoys bad puns, obnoxious pranks. Povis is quite honest.

Scarecrow: HD 4 (18 hp); AC 5 [14]; Atk 2 claws (1d4); Move 9; Save 13; CL/XP 5/240; Special: Fiery breath (5-ft cone, 2d6 damage, save for half), cannot be surprised.

0304.

Hidden among the tall pines there is a large idol carved from the living stone and haunted by dozens of giant ravens that do not take kindly to strangers. The idol looks like a giant, stylized warrior – stocky, with angular features and a long beard. Runic inscriptions around the base read "Seek ye Death in one and one you'll meet its Bride". Naturally, this is reference to the two days of travel, by foot, required to reach the Palace of the Winter Wind in Hex 0402. A secret catch atop the idol opens a concealed door in its back. The door reveals a narrow, winding tunnel that meanders deep into the earth, finally depositing explorers in a small, circular cave of crystal. Immediately upon entering, the explorers will discover that their every thought will flash up on the facets of the crystalline walls – maybe making for awkward or dangerous situations depending on the state of party relations. With concentration (and rolling 4d6 below one's Wisdom score), a viewer can use these crystal facets to see into other dimensions and time – and those scryed upon can see the viewer as well!

0316.

Looking down on the river from a rocky prominence is a wooden tower owned by the arch-witch Addana of the Nine Cats. The tower is constructed in the manner of the stave churches of medieval Norway and houses Adanna, her six apprentices and her nine infamous cats. Addana's apprentices are all maidens taken from the savage tribes of the region as tribute, for all fear her power. Under her tutelage, they become magic-users in their own right and either return to their tribes as wise women or head to greener pastures to pursue a life of adventure. Addana's specialty is summoning, and her nine cats are actually minor daemons in feline form. Each has the abilities of a 3rd level magic-user and 15% magic resistance, as well as the ability to see through magical darkness. The interior of Addana's home is well appointed. The floors and walls are hung with rich pelts and skins, the furniture is all hand carved from fine woods and meticulously oiled and the art objects are all of fine quality. In all, Addana's furnishings are probably worth 2,000 gp. She also keeps a well stocked wine cellar and pantry behind a secret door.

Treasure: 380 sp, 1,310 gp and four pints of jasmine oil in alabaster pomanders (worth 100 gp).

Addana, Magic-User Lvl 9: HP 28; AC 9 [10]; Atk 1 dagger (1d4); Move 12; Save 7 (5 vs. spells); CL/XP 11/1700; Special: Spells (5th). Attractive, rubenesque woman with raven hair that has a silver streak running through it. She wears tasteful gowns of dark velvet and regards everyone with heavy, suspicious eyes. Addana develops powerful, obsessive loves with strong, tall men easily, and if such a PC visits her he may find himself the subject of her undivided attention. Spurning her is only slightly less dangerous than indulging her.

Familiars: HD 1 (HP 6); AC 5 [14]; Atk 1 bite (1d4); Move 15; Save 17; CL/XP 3/60; Special: Spells (3rd), magic resistance 10%, see in darkness.

0323.

A strange clocktower has been carved into the living rock in the side of a wooded butte. The tower is roughly 40 feet wide and 60 feet tall. Although one cannot tell this from the exterior, the interior levels of the clock are roughly 40 to 50 feet deep. The top of the clocktower has a hemispherical opening through which one can see two steel wolves chasing a golden sun or silver moon, depending on whether it is day or night. The tower is inhabited by twenty automatons, spherical brass men with lantern-like eyes and what appear to be long, droopy mustaches of copper wiring hanging from their brazen faces. The leader of the automatons, Godvogot, is a master engineer and tinker who is quite able (and willing) to repair arms and armor and other devices. He and his followers believe in no uncertain terms that their clocktower keeps the universe running. They never allow outsiders into the upper levels of their lair and they fight as though the universe depends on it to protect the machine, which is powered by a subterranean river.

Treasure: 1,550 gp worth of gears, wires, nails, hoops, springs and tools, a jasper worth 700 gp.

Godvogot: HD 7 (31 hp); AC 2 [17]; Atk 1 monkey wrench (1d6) or 1 dart (1d4); Move 9; Save 9; CL/XP 7/600; Special: Immune to sleep and other mind effects, immune to poison, disease and exhaustion.

Automaton: HD 2 (10 hp); AC 2 [17]; Atk 1 tool (1d6) or 1 dart (1d4); Move 9; Save 16; CL/XP 2/30; Special: Immune to sleep and other mind effects, immune to poison, disease and exhaustion.

0402.

Two glacier-carved gorges intersect here, forming the southern boundary of a vast plateau. The plateau's walls are especially rugged and difficult to scale, though the presence of riverine caves suggests that there are subterranean ways to reach the plateau. The top of the plateau appears to be covered with frost all year around. It is inhabited by silver foxes, ravens and owls – all pixies in animal guise that revere and serve the entombed regent of the brilliant castle of blue crystal that lies at the center of the plateau. The strange redoubt, a construction of towering spires, winding corridors and cavernous halls, all freezing to the touch and most inhospitable, is patrolled by winter wolves, howling air elementals and wraiths that resemble gaunt, nearly skeletal women with long hair of Prussian blue wearing flowing robes trimmed with ermine. In its center is the tomb of the Queen of the Winter Winds. Some stories say she is a hibernating demigoddess who will one day awaken and usher in a dark age of perpetual twilight, freezing the rivers and crushing the woodlands beneath mountains of snow. Others believe she was a powerful sorceress who failed in a bid to attain lich-hood, or perhaps placed herself in a deathless sleep to await a fortuitous alignment of the stars. Whatever she might be, a brave and lucky band of adventurers might steal a peek at her, lying in a coffin of ice as translucent as glass. They might be surprised to see her, looking for all the world like a fragile porcelain doll swathed in gauze, human but strangely inhuman in the sharpness of her features and bloodless appearance. The unquiet spirits that lurk in her palace, should one lure them into a conversation, will proclaim that the secret to her wondrous release lies in the south, in the possession of a rival.

Winter Wolf (1d6): HD 5 (HP 25); AC 5 [14]; Atk 1 bite (1d6+1); Move 18; Save 12; CL/XP 6/400; Special: Breathe frost (range 10-ft, 4d6 damage, once per turn).

0414.

When traversing the canyons of this hex, one eventually runs into a great thicket of prickly gooseberry bushes. The green berries are edible, but are extraordinarily tart and benefit greatly from an infusion of sugar. Moving through the thicket takes a full day of cutting and cursing, and the native pixies are quick to hinder one's progress with tricks. Rumor has it that a portal to the land of Fairy lies somewhere in the thicket, either in the form of a talking fountain in which one must drown themselves to make the trip or a large rabbit hole. Before one enters the thicket, they might catch a glimpse of a simple thatched hut belonging to an old Northman named Pasey. Pasey was a scribe and apprentice to the arch-elf Finnin, and claims to have traveled in his youth (a mere three years ago to most folk) into Faerie. He has a weathered tome covered in the hide of a red hart in which he recorded his impressions of the trip, and which folk interested in the court of Faerie and its inhabitants will find invaluable.

Pixie (3d4): HD 1 (HP 5); AC 5 [14]; Atk 1 dagger (1d4) or arrow; Move 6 (F15); Save 17; CL/XP 5/240; Special: Enchanted elfdarts, magic resistance 25%, spells (polymorph self, dancing lights, dispel magic 1/day, permanent confusion 1/ day with successful hit).

0419.

There is a temple of red marble here dedicated to the fire god, whom the Northmen call Sitric. The temple takes the form of nine outer cloisters around a central tower that rises 60 feet high and is topped by an ever-burning beacon. The tower's ground floor is a great temple containing nine bronze pillars bearing glyphs proclaiming the titles of Sitric, such as rapacious devourer, changer of things, watchful eye, etc. In the center of these pillars is a great idol of Sitric, cast in bronze and decorated with gold leaf and fire opals (worth 4,000 gp in all). A sacred flame is kept lit in the idol's open chest, and it is the source of the beacon flame that tops the temple. The upper floors of the temple, accessible through secret doors guarded by halfling priests (see below), contain armories, a rectory, fratry, infirmary and dormitories. The temple is surrounded by a sprawling village of halflings who tend fields of barley, rye and golden potatoes and herd miniature sheep. The halflings separate their fields with prickly hedges of gooseberries. The village boasts a fine roadhouse that serves steaming bowls of potato and barley soup, thick joints of mutton to the big spenders, and both a dark, musky ale and a fine vodka. Fourteen black-robed halflings serve the matriarch of the temple, Tyanna. These halflings can be seen walking through the village, the people bowing to them as they go. Tyanna is currently locked in the infirmary, bound with silver chains, for she contracted lycanthropy while fending off a gang of werewolves less than a month ago. She is desperate or a cure, but her followers are content to be rid of her and are contemplating a more drastic cure for her condition.

Treasure: 1,260 gp and 300 sp kept in a locked iron box in the rectory.

Tyanna, Cleric Lvl 12: HP 46; AC 9 [10] unarmored; Atk 1 mace (1d6); Move 12; Save 5; CL/XP 14/2600; Special: Spells (6th), turn elementals. Owns platemail and shield, but currently unarmored, flanged mace edged with silver, vial of holy water, holy symbol (charred knucklebone in a bronze pendant).

Halfling Priest: HD 1d6; AC 6 [13]; Atk 1 mace (1d6); Move 6; Save 18; CL/XP 1/15; Special: Cast one level 1 cleric spell per day, chanting priests have a 1% chance per halfling of calling down a divine flame from the sky (10' diameter, 6d6 damage, save for half). Leather and shield under black robes, mace, holy symbol, vial of holy water.

0425.

A spring of magical water, bubbling and warm and with a slightly medicinal smell, bursts from the side of a weathered cliff and falls into a basin that has been carved to look like two cupped hands with long fingernails that curl backwards. Bathing in the pool washes away curses, but permanently dyes the skin to match one's moral beliefs – deep red for chaotics, lemon yellow for neutrals and sapphire blue for those of a lawful bent.

0504.

A cleric-turned-wendigo resides in a tall, narrow cave – really more a fissure in a rocky hillside – overlooking the river. By night the priest hunts for prey along the river, but during the day it returns to its lair to pray before a profaned altar and a crudely carved idol that mocks Scarlad, a god of justice that the priest once served. As an anti-cleric, the wendigo retains the ability to cast reverse cleric spells. The wendigo's treasure is heaped around his blood-stained altar.

Treasure: 1,060 sp, 470 gp, and two hematites worth 50 gp each.

Wendigo: HD 4 (14 hp); AC 4 [15]; Atk 1 bite (1d6); Move 15; Save 13; CL/XP 5/240; Special: Immune to cold, only killed by silver or magic weapons – otherwise regenerate 2 hp per turn after "death", reverse cleric spells as a 4th level cleric.

0506.

In a cave about 3 miles south of the river, a large male owlbear has made a lair for itself. The cave is obscured by the surrounding foliage and it contains a disturbing idol of a forgotten god. The deity (or demon) appears to be an unlovely cross between a slug and a bugbear, and is carved from the living rock and painted with ochre. Two tusks jut from the idol's mouth, and the idol's fierce eyes seem to call out to those in search of knowledge. Anyone foolish enough to approach the idol will almost instinctively reach out to touch one of the tusks, and will find it razor sharp. Blood will almost spring from the stricken finger and the victim will lose one level as though their blood were drained by a vampire. In return, a hoarse whispering will echo in their head, revealing to them a future danger. In essence, this knowledge of the future will grant the person a one-time saving throw bonus of +5 to be used during a future crisis.

Owlbear: HD 7+1 (40 hp); AC 5 [14]; Atk 2 claws (1d6), bite (2d6); Move 12; Save 12; CL/XP 7/600; Special: Hug for additional 2d8 if to-hit roll is 18+.

0508.

A family of werewolves dwells here in a lonely cabin in the woods. A more proper wolves den is dug under the cabin, and it is here that they store their treasure and the bones of their victims. The werewolves number three – two males and a seemingly harmless little woman. The men are named Aglor and Duhar and the woman Kelve, and in their human guise they appear to be Northman trappers. Their treasure consists of 670 sp, 670 gp and a pearl worth 2 gp kept in buried leather sacks.

Werewolf: HD 4+4 (27, 18, 16 hp); AC 5 [14]; Atk 1 bite (2d4); Move 12; Save 13; CL/XP 5/240; Special: Lycanthropy, only killed by silver or magic weapons.

0511.

A forested butte hides a sylvan glade and a herd of ten shaggy unicorns. The glade contains a pool of silvery water. The bottom of the pool appears to be glass of silvery blue, and bears the face of the elk goddess Yhoundeh. Bathing in the pool cures minor ills (1d6+2 damage) and soothes the spirit.

0515.

A tribe of 200 goblins dwells here in a dry canyon. They occupy a multi-level complex of caves dug into the walls of the canyon, sharing the complex with a trio of ogres and other subterranean menaces. The goblins are the complex's first line of defense. They wear tanned hides and black hoods, and their king, Morgof, and his six bodyguards (who each have a full hit dice and maximum hit points) ride giant bats into battle. The goblins are known for their archery skill and the madness of their king – he claims to be a polymorphed elf. The goblins keep a treasure of 600 sp and 80 gp, and their king wears a thick leather belt with a brass buckle in the shape of a grimacing lion. The buckle is worth 95 gp.

0603.

An old ship's compass has somehow become lodged in the soil of the forest floor. The compass is made of polished wood, ivory and brass, and would be worth 100 gp if it were not broken – it always points towards DEATH!

0606.

A large log has been felled over the creek here to create a bridge. The banks of the creek here are inhabited by a clutch of fire-breathing toads, the bridge now holding a sample of their handiwork in the form of a pair of smoldering boots that have lost their owner.

Fire-Breathing Toad: HD 3 (HP 15); AC 5 [14]; Atk 1 bite (1d4) or fire; Move 12; Save 14; CL/XP 4/120; Special: Breath a cone of fire 15-ft long and 10-ft wide at base that causes 2d6 damage (save for half).

0612.

A family of dwarves, grey-skinned beings with twinkling amber eyes and hair like Spanish moss, has established a forge here in the woods. The dwarfs keep a large charcoal pit and have cleared a great deal of forest to feed their fires. The forge is a sturdy building of stone blocks, with large double doors allowing heat to escape and air and light to enter. The forge is surrounded by a stone cottage and a large, wooden storage shed. The storage shed not only holds tools, fuel and raw materials; it is also the entrance to a small iron mine. The dwarves number eight, the heads of the family being old Beotem and his goodwife Guind (a genius at etching). They have three adult children, Osgil, Yarmithe and Waltla, all excellent smiths, and four younger children, all apprentices in the shop. Beotem is a fat, old dwarf and the finest smith of the family, being able to produce magical weaponry and armor if given the proper ingredients and enough time. Beotem is a hard fellow to get along with – he is a perfectionist and egotist, and more than a few people have left his forge with a dent in their heads. All of the dwarves should be treated as dwarf warriors for the purpose of combat, with Beotem having the ability to enchant items as though he were a 11th level magic-user.

0617.

Four square blocks, about 30- tall, wide and high rest here in the middle of a wide river ford. The blocks are placed in a square formation with about 10 feet between each of them. Each block is composed of black stone that shines purple in the sunlight and a luminous topaz in the moonlight, and they are completely immune to magical and non-magical probing of any kind save teleportation. The blocks compose an ancient tomb of a great warlord and shaman of the hivernians. Each block has a 20x20 room hidden inside of it, with portals connecting it to two other blocks. Attempts to teleport from the a block fails 20% of the time, with failures sending the mage into a random block.

Block A is always the first block entered, regardless of where the spellcaster aims his or her teleportation. It is a gloomy room hung with bark cloth curtains died deep maroon. A small table of white stone rests in the middle of the room and is inlaid with representations of elks and flames in amber (about 100 gp worth). Sitting on the table is a silver flagon of purple dust and an onyx bowl containing a conical candle of green wax. Two copper goblets complete the set (each piece worth about 10 gp). Should adventurers pour the purple dust into the goblets and clink them together, they will be teleported to Block B (with the goblets). Should adventurers light the candle, the greenish smoke that billows from it will send them reeling and deposit them in Block C.

Block B is a shrine dedicated to the ancient goddess Yhoundeh. It contains an idol of the grim goddess composed of a human skeleton dipped in wax, giving it a pallid, translucent "skin" and wearing a triangular bronze headdress surmounted with elk antlers. The idol holds a goblet of unholy water in its left hand and a leather scourge in the right. A dagger, glowing crimson, is placed within the idol's rib cage, and a dozen clay bowls containing various pigments, litter the floor. The walls are blank and greyish-white. Painting the a dagger, goblet or scourge on a wall teleports adventurers to Block A. Painting all three in the correct order (scourge-dagger-goblet) teleports adventurers to Block D. Painting all three in the wrong order summons an Aerial Servant who quickly moves to dispatch the heretics.

Block C is a guard house of sorts. On the east and west walls there are armored skeletons, leaf-bladed short swords wired into their hands, bodies secured to the wall with leather straps. On the north and south walls there are mosaics made with colored shells. One depicts a pounding surf at sunset while the other a blue-skinned amazon in a long, red, buckskin dress wearing a headdress surmounted by elk antlers. This amazon is standing amidst tongues of flame and her eyes appear to be torn out, the sockets running red with blood. Should one cut themselves on a skeletal warrior's sword and place his bloody hand on the mosaic of the elk-goddess, they will be teleported to Block D. Should they do the same to the mosaic of the beach, they will be blasted by a cone of cold (4d6 damage) and deposited in Block B.

Block D is the last resting place of Ghzirdoz, a high priest of Yhoundeh that died well over 1,000 years ago. The high priest's slab consists of four bars of bronze stretched from one side of the chamber to the other, with the body placed atop these bars. Touching the bars with one's bare hand forces a saving throw – those who fail cannot remove their hands from the bar they touch, and they will feel their soul slowly leaving their body through their fingers. The soul will migrate to the body on the slab, causing it to awaken, hover above the bars and attack for one round per level of the soul-sapped victim, whose body now lies alive but inanimate on the floor. At this point, the body will collapse back onto the bars and a death mask of purple stone will appear on a random wall. The mask will resemble the true soul of the victim – angelic and calm if benevolent, twisted and monstrous if wicked. Placing a mask on a victim will re-animate the body for 1 hour per day, but no more. Stronger magic is required to return soul to body. If the high priest's body is destroyed while it is animated, the victim's soul will return to his body without harm and the floor of the block will disappear, sending adventures falling into a lightless void, only to soon come to laying on the roof of the stone block, each holding a tiger's eye gem worth 500 gp. These gems allow their possessors to communicate with one another via telepathy.

0621.

Two giant ravens have made a home here in the branches of a giant beech. The tree is inhabited by a sisterhood of five dryads. The ravens are notorious thieves, and have amassed a small treasure in their nest. **Treasure:** Moonstone worth 105 gp, two obsidian spearheads worth 400 gp (and is +1 to hit for the first five attacks it makes due to its razor sharpness), hematite worth 1 gp, a brass toe ring worth 800 gp and rose quartz toad worth 4 gp.

Giant Raven: HD 3 (HP 15); AC 5 [14]; Atk 1 bite (1d8); Move 2 (F20); Save 14; CL/XP 4/240; Special: None.

Dryads: HD 2 (HP 10); AC 9 [10]; Atk 1 wooden dagger (1d4); Move 12; Save 16; CL/XP 3/60; Special: Charm person (-2 to save).

0701.

A spiny green dragon with forest green scales lives here in a hollow beneath a large tree. The dragon is called Zexter and is more mellow and friendly than most of its ilk, though only in relative terms. Zexter can speak but cannot use magic. He is small and immature and is more likely to flee an attack and stalk the adventurers in hopes of gaining revenge than standing and fighting to the death.

Zexter: HD 7 (21 hp); AC 2 [17]; Atk 2 claws (1d6) and 1 bite (2d10); Move 9 (F24); Save 9; CL/XP 9/1100; Special: Breathes a cloud of poisonous gas 50' in diameter.

0705.

The river narrows here and becomes a series of rapids that spray the granite banks and feed a flourishing crop of thick vines with fragrant, ruby-black blossoms. The blossoms, harvested under a new moon with a silver blade, can be brewed into a tea that cures lycanthropy. The werewolves of the Winter Woods know about these blossoms, and have set a number of shallow, spiked pits along the shore to catch would-be harvesters. The blooms open only at night, and the heady fragrance they emit can cause terrible hallucinations (saving throw to avoid).

0709.

Artain is a small village of shepherds. The village consists of about 60 small, wooden huts protected by a wooden stockade, itself surrounded by a deep moat filled with wooden spikes tipped with wolvesbane. A wooden causeway crosses the moat and leads to a stone moat house, the sturdiest building in the village and fancy enough that it must surely have been built by other folk. The iron portcullis of the moat house is covered with at least 300 silver coins that have been affixed by nails, apparently in an attempt to make the thing unpleasant to lycanthropes. The people of Artain are predominantly Northmen, but they appear to have mixed with the native population, for their skin is a light yellow-brown and their facial features rougher than the average Northman's. A large, wooden house is constructed abutting the moat house, and this serves as the home of the village's leader, a dark-visaged elf called Abethelm, and his retainers, a brooding band of warriors in dark leathers. The warriors, ten in number, wear silver holy symbols and carry silver daggers and several silver-tipped arrows in their quivers, besides their light crossbows and short swords. Nocturnal travelers might well run into a patrol of these warrior and discover, to their terror, that they attack first and ask questions later, disappearing back into their night if their ambush proves unsuccessful. Abethelm and his people pray to Xevus, a patron saint of travelers. A large, wooden idol of the god has been erected in the village square next to the moat house and Abethelm's home, and daily calls to prayer are headed by all in the village save the shepherds grazing their flocks by the riverside meadows. Xevus appears as a tall, blue-skinned man with four arms, hawk wings and a feathered head.

Abethelm, Elf Lvl 5: HD 5d6+10 or 5d6-5; AC 9 [10] or 1 [18]; Save 10/11 (9 vs. spells); CL/XP 6/400; Special: Magic-user spells (3rd).

Warriors (10), Thieves Lvl 3: HD 3d6; AC 7 [12]; Save 13 (11 vs. devices); CL/XP 3/60; Special: Thief skills, backstab (+4 to hit, x2 damage).

0714.

In a wide canyon there is a great mound of white earth and stones, clearly raised by human (or humanoid) hands. Standing atop this hill is a statue of an avenging angel, four wings outstretched, sword at

side, one arm outstretched and grasping a torch. A wooden platform has been erected beneath this outstretched hand, and close inspection will reveal a bit of rope secured to the wrist – it would seem this statue has been used as a gallows. Dozens of shallow graves dot the area around the mound, all of them marked with a wooden stake and a wreath of wolvesbane (usually dry). One grave has been disturbed and is surrounded by wolf tracks.

0806.

An unassuming cave in the side of a butte is the entrance to an old iron mine. The mine was worked by kobolds, who excavated a number of "living tunnels" as well as mine shafts. The slope that leads up to the mine entrance is marred by dozens of slag heaps and clay furnaces. Inside the mine adventurers will discover a terrible slaughter – more than a hundred kobolds (including females and young) killed, apparently by wolf attack. A secret door in the large communal chamber at the end of the entrance tunnel leads to a vertical passage 200-ft deep. At the bottom of this passage there is a vast limestone vault that holds a pristine subterranean lake inhabited by blind fish, glowing spiders and a tribe of pale nixies. The survivors of the kobold slaughter can also be found here, led by their chieftain Glixtik. The small band of thirty kobolds, including 8 females and 11 young, is in no mood for a fight, and may even beg for protection if they sense a lawful person among the adventurers. They are aware of the flowers in 0705 and are aware that the forces of the Queen of the Winter Wind are preparing for her return. The kobolds shirked their tribute to the Queen and were summarily punished.

0811.

A band of twenty bandits has established itself on a rocky promontory, erecting short walls of stone and wood to supplement their rocky perch. The bandits all have sepia colored skin, shaggy, reddish-brown hair, black eyes and long, pointed chins, and most magic-users will be able to identify them as vat-grown men. They wear ring mail and carry long pole axes. Atop their rocky lair they dwell in leather tents and keep their wealth in leather sacks, some of which contain hissing spiders as protection from thieves (treat as poisoned needle, death comes in 1d6 turns). Assume that each bandit has 4d6 gp in treasure.

Vat-Grown Bandit: HD 2 (HP 10); AC 6 [13]; Atk 1 weapon (1d10); Move 12; Save 16; CL/XP 2/30; Special: Go berserk when reduced to half hit points, gaining one additional attack each round.

0814.

Passage through a narrow canyon (roughly 40-ft wide) is blocked by a keep that stretches from one wall to the other. The keep is 50 feet tall and forms a bridge from mesa to mesa, a bridge blocked by a gatehouse always staffed by three warriors wearing chainmail hauberks and helms affixed with raven wings. These stout warriors carry shields and swords and charge a toll of 10 gp per person. The bridge and keep are 30-ft wide. It can be entered through a secret trap door in the gatehouse above, or via a double set of iron doors at the base of the construction on either side of it. The keep has 10-ft thick walls and a stone interior that looks to have been designed and built by dwarfs. The keep's present owner, the barbaric warrior woman Cwelfalys, maintains 40 men-at-arms, 8 elite warriors, a court mage and shaman and perhaps a three dozen attendants, including musicians. Cwelfalys cut a red road of slaughter through the Winter Woods before seizing the keep a decade ago from a lord of the Northmen whose skull still decorates her throne. She has cleared the surrounding area of bandits and monsters, and is said to be biding her time before she calls the winter tribes to her green dragon banner and drives the Northmen out of the Winter Woods forever.

Treasure: 710 sp, 690 gp, a chyrsoprase worth 2,000 gp and an alabaster dish studded with precious stones worth 1,350 gp.

Cwlfalys, Fighting-Woman Lvl 10: HP 68; AC 4 [15]; Save 5;

CL/XP 10/1400. Chainmail, double-bladed axe, wolf-skin cape worth 30 gp. A brooding woman, thickly muscled and grim countenanced. Her hair is braided and decorated with silver combs worth 100 gp.

Kelvi, Magic-User Lvl 3: HP 7; AC 9 [10]; Save 13 (11 vs. spells); CL/XP 4/120; Special: Spells (2nd). Staff, dagger. Upright, broad-shouldered man (+1 strength bonus) with curly auburn hair and twinkling eyes. Dresses like a woodsman.

Iarthildam, Cleric Lvl 5: HP 23; AC 3 [16]; Save 11 (9 vs. paralysis and poison); CL/XP 6/400; Special: Spells (3rd), rebuke undead. Gangling, wicked man with tufts of wispy grey hair over each ear and narrow, pink eyes.

0817.

A pack of fifteen werewolves lairs here in the cellar (and former torture chamber) of a crumbling donjon, the upper portions having fallen into a pile of charred stone. One of them is Wallauna, daughter of the warrior-crone in Hex 0824. Wallauna is now a werewolf and quite happy with her new found power. Given enough warning, the werewolves might use her to lure would-be rescuers into an ambush.

Treasure: 1,420 sp, 2,470 gp and a parchment scroll containing the spells Cure Disease and Silence, 15'-radius.

Werewolf: HD 4+4 (HP 24); AC 5 [14]; Atk 1 bite (2d4); Move 12; Save 13; CL/XP 5/240; Special: Lycanthropy, only killed by silver or magic weapons.

0824.

Overlooking the Great River here is the immense castle of Hiceleth, the so-called "Iron Crone". Hiceleth is a northern woman of 70 winters wearing a perpetual scowl and suspicious eyes. Hiceleth was a magnificent warrior in her day, but now relies on her force of personality and genius for strategy and tactics to keep her subjects loyal. Hiceleth's castle is a towering keep of black stone with four great towers. The keep is surrounded by a tall wall of black stone that protects not only the keep, but also a large village of narrow, winding lanes and tall, wattle-and-daub townhouses. Outside the walls are acres and acres of uneven, rocky uplands that divide irregularly shaped wheat fields, meadows dotted with fat, white sheep and orchards of linden trees. The domain is patrolled by Hiceleth's elite cavaliers, fifteen veteran warriors in black armor carrying lances, shields and long swords, their fifteen mounted squires in chainmail and carrying shields, long swords and light crossbows. Three mangonels in stone redoubts command the Great River, persuading most river traffic to come ashore and pay a toll. To say Hiceleth is not well liked is to make a distinct understatement, but she is feared and respected, and with the collapse of the Northmen's empire to the east, many look to her to forge a new kingdom. Unfortunately, Hiceleth is too preoccupied with the disappearance of her daughter, Wallauna (see Hex 0817). In addition to her cavaliers and their squires, Hiceleth commands 50 men-at-arms equipped with ring armor, shield, spear and short bow. She is advised by a mage who calls himself Osmayeven of the Sundered Beard.

Treasure: 7,000 sp, 1,000 gp.

Hiceleth, Fighting-Woman Lvl 11: HP 43; AC 10 [9] or 3 [16] in platemail with shield; Save 4; CL/XP 11/1700; Special: Old age has given her a -1 penalty in Str, Dex and Con. Miserly old woman, dressed in gowns of dark, nearly black scarlet and wears a golden crown. She keeps her sword and shield nearby, just in case.

Osmayeven, Magic-User Lvl 5: HP 13; AC 9 [10]; Save 11 (9 vs. spells); CL/XP 6/400; Special: Spells (3rd). Black, forked beard, flushed face, mocking smile. Osmayeven is a lazy libertine, but politically astute and ambitious.

0904.

On a windswept mesa pocked with tiny pools of freezing water there is a pavilion of living, braided yew trees woven so thickly that not a ray of sunlight can penetrate the interior. Inside the pavilion there is a coffin of crystalline steel, and within the coffin there is a magnificent silver sword. The sword has a starburst hilt, and motes of light can be seen meandering up and down the blade, which seems to emit an audible moan. The coffin appears to be immune to any and all attempts to force it open – in fact, closer inspection reveals it as more of a cocoon than a box, with no apparent seam denoting a lid. The coffin can be opened, but only by the following means: Using mirrors, one (well, two actually) must reflect an image of both the full moon and the sun on the coffin's surface at the same time. Obviously, this can only be accomplished on days when the moon is both full and in the sky during daylight hours. Should this be accomplished, the coffin will shatter. The sword can be claimed by any person, and when grasped will grow over the person's hand like a gauntlet and never let go. The sword has a powerful ego, and it will demand its wielder take on the mantle of the Star Maiden's champion (though who the Star Maiden is only sages and clerics well versed in pre-human mythology can tell). The sword is +1/+3 vs undead. It moans softly when it cannot see the stars and can produce a protection from evil, 10' radius effect once per day.

0906.

A creepy hermit lives in the tangled woods here, having constructed a hovel of branches and skins and partially dug into the earth. The hermit calls himself Nessel, but those who have crossed his path refer to him as the "Spider Eater", for he makes a feast of insects. Nessel uses sprigs of wolvesbane around his hovel to keep away the werewolves, who, truth be told, have little desire to visit the odd little man who saves his nail clippings, hair and peeled skin in clay pots. Nessel is not evil, merely eccentric and disturbing in the extreme, and he welcomes visitors into his home for short periods. He has a good knowledge of the land north of the river.

0920.

Much of the lake shore here is covered by a long, thin strand of field stone cottages belonging to fishermen. The village, called Sammothiro, is protected by a tall rampart studded with pit traps that deposit victims into nets and patrolled by diligent crossbowmen and, in the skies above, trained giant falcons. The falcons are primarily used to fish the lake, but a few of the more intelligent birds are trained to alert the villagers of potential invaders. The Sammothirans themselves hunt the giant pike that roam Lake Gaurh. Massive fish, the operation is not unlike whaling in its process and danger. Sammothiro is ruled by Jonaldur, a sheriff appointed by the Prince of Yaryg, a fortified town to the east that still holds power in the region. Northmen by blood and culture, the Sammothirans are known for their use of fish bones in their art and their skill with spear and harpoon. Besides their cottages and Jonaldur's manor, the village also boasts a temple dedicated to Gaurh, the god of the lake, a beacon tower and a fine, old inn much visited by the locals for its crawfish stew, thick crackers and a spicy liqueur brewed from tree bark. The inn usually has rooms available for visitors, but they are locked from the outside until dawn due to a werewolf problem in the region.

Jonaldur, Fighter Lvl 4: HP 21; AC 4 [15]; Save 11; CL/XP 4/120. Chainmail, shield, battle axe, hand axe. Pudgy, long face, secretive and wilful. Only family is an elderly aunt living in Yaryg, a half-sister to the Prince.

Uilice, Cleric Lvl 2: HP 9; AC 7 [12]; Save 14 (12 vs. paralysis and poison); CL/XP 3/60; Special: Spells (1st), turn undead. Cursed leather -1, shield, mace, holy symbol. Slight build, broad, oval face with clueless eyes. Tends to be lax in his duties. Wears cursed leather he cannot remove – the words "Kick Me" are embossed on the back in large, gold letters, so he's always in

his priestly robe. Also wears a brass ring worth 15 gp.

1005.

A blood-sucking lamia with the upper torso of an alabaster-skinned beauty and the body of a grizzly bear dwells in a high cave, the ground outside it littered with animal and humanoid bones. Ten animated skeletons lurk beneath these bones. The lamia's entire treasure consists of thirteen hourglasses of various makes and models, but worth about 100 gp each. She is currently without slaves, having just finished the last one a few days ago.

Lamia: HD 9; AC 3 [16]; Atk 2 claws (1d6); Move 24; Save 6; CL/XP 12/2000; Special: Spells, touch drains wisdom.

Skeletons: HD 1 (HP 5); AC 8 [11]; Atk 1 club (1d6); Move 12; Save 17; CL/XP 1/15; Special: None.

1011.

Greenstone Abbey is dedicated to Forda, the Northmen's goddess of agriculture. It is, in effect, an attempt by the forces of growth and Spring to colonize a woodland once under the sway of the forces of Winter, and in that regard it presents a tempting target for the revitalized forces of the Queen of the Winter Wind. The abbey is under the governance of Sandragorn, a statuesque man with thick, mutton-chop sideburns of white hair that stand out on his dark brown skin. Sandragorn despises ignorance and does his best to live a useful, virtuous life – but he has developed a strange fascination with Hiceleth in Hex 0824. Sandragorn's monks, who number twelve, are warrior-priests who wear green robes over chainmail and carry thick cudgels (1d4+1 damage) and large, leather-bound almanacs from which they often quote parcels of Forda's wisdom. The abbey is built in an L-shape on a similarly shaped ridge, and can only be gained by climbing a narrow stair or via barrels and pulleys (used to bring supplies into the monastery). The land around the abbey has been cleared of brush and trees and is worked daily by the fifty lay brethren of the abbey, all pilgrims from the east who, advised that the end was near, trekked into the Winter Woods to find salvation through toil. The fields around the abbey grow barley, apples, pumpkins, hazelnuts, borage, peppermint, hemp, spelt, fiddleheads and parsnips.

Sandragorn, Cleric Lvl 10: HP 57; AC 2 [17]; Save 6 (4 vs. paralysis and poison); CL/XP 12/2000; Special: Spells (5th), turn undead. Platemail (lacquered green), shield bearing an image of Forda, mace, holy symbol. Forda is short and wide of hip, with narrow red eyes and white skin in robes of green leaves and vines and carrying a gourd. Clerics of Forda can cause crops to ripen with their touch.

Beadles of Forda (7), Clerics Lvl 1: HD 1 (HP 5); AC 5 [14]; Save 15 (13 vs. paralysis and poison); CL/XP 1/15; Special: Turn undead. Chainmail, leather book, cudgel, holy symbol.

Almoners of Forda (4), Clerics Lvl 2: HD 2 (HP 10); AC 5 [14]; Save 14 (12 vs. paralysis and poison); CL/XP 3/60; Special: Spells (1st), turn undead. Chainmail, leather book, cudgel, holy symbol.

Chanters of Forda (1), Clerics Lvl 3: HD 3 (HP 15); AC 5 [14]; Save 13 (11 vs. paralysis and poison); CL/XP 4/120; Special: Spells (1st), turn undead. Chainmail, leather book, cudgel, holy symbol.

1018.

Perched on a platform in a tall tree lives Kabranornen, sagacious oracle of the Winter Wood and favorite of lords, ladies and woodsmen alike. Kabranornen is especially sensitive to loud noises, and thus prefers to dwell in the middle of nowhere attended only by his beloved carrier pigeons and a pet spider named Loop. Most of the villages and strong-holds in the neighborhood keep one or more of his pigeons, sending requests for advice, knowledge and prophecy to him by securing notes to the pigeon's legs. Sometimes Kabranornen replies, other times he does not.

Treasure: A magic book of never-ending stories and a pair of spectacles that, when commanded with the word "Gerfluff" allow Kabranornen to see in darkness, see invisible creatures, use x-ray vision or comprehend languages. This effect lasts 1 hour and can be done but once per day.

Kabranornen, Magic-User Lvl 9: HP 22; AC 9 [10]; Save 7 (5 vs. spells); CL/XP 11/1700; Special: Spells (5th). Grey-haired, grey-eyed, rotund with a small, puckered face. Lazy and flirtatious.

1025.

Night-time travelers in this hex may (3 in 6 chance) be witness to a fearful spectacle. From the folds of Nix's robes will emerge thirteen dead revelers, rotting and skeletal with loose gibbets of meat hanging from the bones and crashing tambourines in their hands. They caper and dance like young men and women, but their laughs and cries of merriment are hoarse and whispery. They will insist the adventurers join their dance, and those who do will discover them good, though grisly, company. If one can dance the entire night through, they will see their cadaverous comrades disappear with the rising of the sun, and will be left with a tambourine that, when played, acts as a protection from evil, 10' radius spell. Should one not be able to keep dancing (make a saving throw or make a constitution check), they will be trampled by the revelers for 1d6 damage and left to rest. If attacked, the revelers turn into wraiths and show no mercy. If ignored, they will go on their way.

Wraith: HD 4 (HD 20); AC 3 [16]; Atk 1 touch (1d6 + level drain); Move 9 (Fly 24); Save 13; CL/XP 6/400; Special: Drain 1 level with hit, only harmed by magic weapons and silver weapons (half damage).

1110. A steaming grotto in the side of a grey, mossy canyon wall is home to five crane maidens. The seven maidens are nymphs, daughters of the river, who can assume the form of stately cranes and command the creatures of the woods and river, in effect summoning 1d6 wolves, 1d3 giant badgers or skunks or 1 brown bear to their aid. The crane maidens generally relax in their natural sauna, venturing out every so often in crane or maiden form, the latter wearing nothing but feathered cloaks. Naturally, in this form they easily attract male attention, and sometimes dally with human beings to relieve their boredom. Several heroes of the hivernians are said to be the issue of such dalliances.

Crane Maiden: HD 3 (HP 15); AC 9 [10]; Atk none; Move 12; Save 14; CL/XP 5/240; Special: Sight causes blindness or death if desired by the maiden, shapechange into crane, summon animals.

1113.

A patrol of 20 goblin wolf riders is camped here, keeping an eye on the Abbey in Hex 1011. The goblins wear long, pointed red caps and red, deerskin coats. They are armed with keen cleavers (treat as battle axes) and short bows. They have 80 gp between them and their leader Trom has a potion of healing.

1115.

Even in the brightest day, the rift that runs through this hex is always shrouded in impenetrable shadow. The rift is really a broad valley, the walls of the valley being a mere 500 feet tall and gentle. Within this weird, shadow realm there is a stone castle inhabited by a shadow king and his court. King Ottin and his people were cursed in ancient times to never again see the sun or feel its warmth. Their valley is now barren save for phosphorescent mosses that grow on stones and equally phosphorescent harts that lap up the moss and provide a measure of sport for the benighted people of the vale. King Ottin's court includes 20 other shadows, four of them knights and

one of them the keeper of a kennel of six shadow mastiffs. For those whose eyes can pierce the darkness, Ottin and his people will be seen to have a ghastle pallor, sharp blue-green eyes, noble faces with delicate features and long hair of black or burnished bronze. They dress in tunics of scarlet and striped hose, their clothing covered with corded brocades. Ottin's knights wear blue-black platemail and ride black stallions in chainmail barding. They wield large, curved swords and carry shields emblazoned with a black sun on a grey field. The people of the Valley cannot leave it, for to see or feel the sun would mean their doom. The shadow people fear the sight of gold, and its touch causes 1d4 damage to them per round.

Treasure: 13,000 coins of black bronze (e.g. copper pieces), moss agate worth 60 gp and a wand of rope trick with 2 charges.

Ottin, Shadow Fighter Lvl 8: HP 57; AC 2 [17]; Save 7; CL/XP 9/1100; Special: Drains 1 Str with hit, can only be hit by magic or golden weapons, immune to sleep and charm. Tall, overly proud, devoid of mercy.

Shadow Knight: HD 5+5 (HP 30); AC 2 [17]; Atk 1 weapon (1d8) or touch (1d4 + Str drain); Move 12; Save 12; CL/XP 6/400; Special: Drains 1 Str with hit, can only be hit by magic or golden weapons, immune to sleep and charm.

Shadow: HD 3+3 (HP 18); AC 7 [12]; Atk 1 touch (1d4 + Str drain); Move 12; Save 14; CL/XP 4/120; Special: Drains 1 Str with hit, can only be hit by magic or golden weapons, immune to sleep and charm.

Shadow Mastiff: HD 3 (HP 15); AC 6 [13]; Atk 1 bite (1d6+1); Move 18; Save 14; CL/XP 5/240; Special: Baying (save or drop everything and flee for 3d6 turns), 40% concealment in shadow.

1203.

A gang of fifteen hill giants occupy a large hall made of rough-cut timber. The hall has a single, massive room with a 10-ft diameter fire pit in its center. Benches and piles of furs litter the room, and giant weaponry and hunting trophies, including a festive garland of human skulls, decorate the walls. The hill giants are eating, sleeping, brawling or maintaining their armor and weapons when encountered. Besides the 15 males, there are 8 females who fight as ogres and 10 children who fight as bugbears. The children are usually mending things, cutting firewood or doing other manual labors, and the females are making clothes from furs or cooking – roasting a cow over the fire pit, brewing spruce tip tea or making greasy porridge. Dug into the area surrounding the hall are a dozen pits covered with lids made of several tree trunks strung together with leather thongs. These pits are about 10-ft deep and not designed as traps. Rather, they are used to store salted meats, barrels of roots and casks of mead, ale, wine and anything else the giants have stolen from human settlements to the south. One pit is used for captives, and there is a 1 in 6 chance that it is occupied by 1d6 humans taken from a caravan or the outskirts of a village. The humans will be in rough shape, but capable of moving under their own power. The chief of the giants is called Plach.

Treasure: 3,800 sp, 7,740 gp, silver statuette of the Queen of the Winter Wind worth 800 gp, nine sable skins (worth 10 gp each) and a brass tiara, slightly dented and being worn on a leather necklace by a giantess, worth 115 gp.

Plach, Hill Giant Chief: HD 8+2 (46 hp); AC 3 [16]; Atk 1 weapon or boulder (2d10); Move 12; Save 8; CL/XP 9/1100; Special: Throw boulders.

Hill Giants: HD 8+2 (HP 42); AC 4 [15]; Atk 1 weapon or boulder (2d8); Move 12; Save 8; CL/XP 9/1100; Special: Throw boulders.

1309.

A small dispatch of fifteen bandy-legged hobgoblins from Hex

1319 has made camp here. The hobgoblins wear tunics of ring armor and carry pole arms and short bows. Each hobgoblin has learned the art of riding a giant boar using only their knees to guide the beast, making them especially dangerous. The commander of the expedition is called Juvash, and he is notable for his missing ear and oversized fangs, which give him a lisp that his soldiers are at great pains to ignore.

Juvash: HD 3+3 (HP 18); AC 4 [15]; Atk 1 weapon (1d10 or 1d6); Move 9; Save 14; CL/XP 3/60; Special: None.

Hobgoblin: HD 1+1 (HP 6); AC 5 [14]; Atk 1 weapon (1d10 or 1d6); Move 9; Save 17; CL/XP 1/15; Special: None.

Giant Boar: HD 4+4 (HP 24); AC 6 [13]; Atk 1 gore (3d6); Move 15; Save 13; CL/XP 5/240; Special: Continues attacking two rounds after death.

1323.

The Northmen have established a large fishing village here called Xalter. Xalter is a village of whitewashed wattle-and-daub homes with doors painted in bright, rainbow patterns. The village is surrounded by a similarly painted wooden palisade and is situated on a crescent shaped island in the middle of the Sable River. Stone watch towers on either end of the island provide additional security. The people of Xalter are almost uniformly handsome, with amethyst eyes, chiseled faces and slight overbites and lisps. The village is dominated by two large buildings, facing each other across a cobblestone-paved plaza. The first is a two-story building of stone and wood that serves as the manor of the village's mayor, Nogan, a gruff old sinner who lost an eye in a knife fight. Nogan is a bit thuggish, but has the best interests of his village at heart. The other large building inside the village walls is a stone temple coated in stucco, painted a brilliant vermillion and surmounted by a copper dome. This is the temple of Uchai, goddess of river otters. The rocky coastline of Xalter's island are decorated with sculptures of selkies, and Uchai's temple is actually built atop partially submerged limestone caverns where selkies sometimes congregate to receive gifts from Uchai's high priest, Peribal, and other high members of her cult. Uchai's rites run toward the bawdy, and wine-fueled celebrations occur throughout the year. Aside from the mayor's residence and the temple, the most astonishing construction in Xalter is its tavern, a long, wooden building with a gabled roof (and lofts that can be rented by the hour or the night) standing on stilts about 10 yards off the shore of the island. The tavern is connected to the island by a causeway and is known for its eel and cheddar pies and its fortified wines.

Peribal, Cleric Lvl 3: HP 11; AC 3 [16] when armored; Save 13 (11 vs. paralysis and poison); CL/XP 4/120; Special: Cleric spells (1st), turn undead. Chainmail, shield, mace, the flanges stylized in the shape of enticing selkies with arched backs. Curly hair, slight, graceful features. Forgetful and often over-zealous in his exuberance for Uchai.

1404.

A herd of sixteen mastodons is encamped in this hex, its matron having been injured during an ill-fated hobgoblin attack. The creatures are on high alert and agitated, and attack at the slightest provocation.

Mastodon: HD 12 (HP 60); AC 6 [13]; Atk 1 trunk (1d10), 2 gore (1d10), 2 trample (2d6); Move 12; Save 3; CL/XP 13/2300; Special: None.

1503.

The grasses in this hex are a pale, sickly yellow in color. Within an hour of entering the hex, one will begin to notice skeletons of small creatures, and their throats will feel parched. If they turn back now, they should lose a mere 1d6 hit points to thirst (reducing the damage by 1 point for every gallon of water consumed). Otherwise, they will begin to lose 1d6 hit points per hour. As they work their way into the hex, larger skeletons will appear. In the center of the hex there is a statue of the Queen of the Winter Wind carved from pure, white alabaster. The Queen appears as a slight humanoid in a crumpled dress. The face is nearly human or elven, but off, somehow, with a slit mouth and eyes that cause a slight nausea in those who stare too long. In all, the image gives the impression of being in the world, but not of the world and passively hostile to the very idea of warmth and joy and passions noble or base.

1415.

A family of three werebears has established a cozy den for itself in a cave beneath a tall alder tree. The cave is a homey affair – knit rugs, cave paintings, a fire pit and three comfortable chairs lined with wolf pelts. Dried meats hang in the back of the cave next to a cupboard holding wooden dishes, bowls and utensils, dried herbs (some medicinal) and jars of blueberry and cranberry preserves and honey. Just down the hill from the cave there are thick tangles of blueberry bushes and three bee hives maintained by the werebears. The werebears are cautiously hospitable if a group of adventurers "smells right", but they are quick to rile if they feel even remotely threatened.

Werebear: HD 7+3 (HP 38); AC 2 [17]; Atk 2 claws (1d3), 1 bite (2d4); Move 9; Save 9; CL/XP 8/800; Special: Lycanthropy.

1418.

A wizened old elf warlock named Uilin dwells in this hex in a stately manor of reddish-grey brick with a gabled roof of black slates. The windows of the manor are barred and are all composed of stained glass in a random, patchwork pattern. The interior of the house is grand but understated. The dozens of small, square rooms are filled with fine furnishings that, despite their splendid design, look old and faded. Uilin is a homely elf, with overlong legs and arms and a squat torso. He usually wears a saffron robe tied with a belt of blue dragon skin. The manor is staffed by intelligent animals – dogs, cats, ferrets and the like – all victims of polymorph and all cowed by their master, for although Uilin seems harmless, he is quite the opposite. Uilin knows of the Queen of the Winter Winds inevitable return – he knows she stalks the maze of canyons in Hex 1513, he believes her triumph over vitality is also inevitable and he intends to share in that triumph. To that end, he has been fashioning a wand of cold for himself and marshalling the region's giants, goblins and hobgoblins, using his apprentices as envoys. The six apprentices are fearful and quiet, and protected by murders of ravens on their journeys into the wilderness.

Treasure: 2,600 sp, 2,200 gp, two opals worth 5,000 gp each and a silver pinky ring worth 750 gp – the ring is a knotwork silver band with a lock of golden hair interwoven with the metal.

Uilin, Elf Magic-User Lvl 10: HP 29; AC 9 [10]; Save 6 (4 vs. spells); CL 12/2000; Special: Spells (5th). Robes, silver dagger, spellbook.

1507.

A tribe of 130 hobgoblins has set up camp in this hex. The camp is composed of 80 or so leather teepees painted with chaos glyphs and runes in the blood of vanquished foes. The bandy-legged hobgoblins have faces of deep purple, long, jutting canine teeth, yellow, cat-like eyes and bristly black hair. The warriors wear leather and ring armor and carry shields painted orange and covered with white hand prints – one for each foe the warrior has killed. The tribe also includes 100 females, 170 young, 250 human slaves (all in miserable condition, with their legs chained to allow halting movement) and sixty giant boars that serve as steeds. The hobgoblins milk the swine, using the curdled, fermented milk as their chief beverage. The tribe is led by a shaman called Nulg, a devotee of the Queen of the Winter Wind. Nulg is assisted by nineteen sub-chiefs who go about wearing only a fur loincloth, wield two-handed swords and go berserk in combat.

Nurg: HD 3+3 (20 hp); AC 4 [15]; Atk 1 weapon (1d6); Move 9; Save 14; CL/XP 4/120; Special: Cast spells as a 5th level cleric.

Sub-Chiefs: HD 1+1 (HP 6); AC 7 [12]; Atk 1 weapon (1d10); Move 9; Save 17; CL/XP 2/30; Special: Go berserk in combat, gaining an additional attack, immune to fear.

Hobgoblin: HD 1+1 (HP 6); AC 5 [14]; Atk 1 weapon (1d10 or 1d6); Move 9; Save 17; CL/XP 1/15; Special: None.

Giant Boar: HD 4+4 (HP 24); AC 6 [13]; Atk 1 gore (3d6); Move 15; Save 13; CL/XP 5/240; Special: Continues attacking two rounds after death.

1513.

As one moves deeper into this hex, they find themselves in a maze-like series of canyons, with streams that seem to flow one way and then another and canyon walls that become more and more towering as one continues to wander. The entire hex is a sort of mystic trap, and one can wander in it without ever escaping. There are, of course, two ways out. The first is to die. The second is to come upon the Maiden of the Maze. Each day spent in the hex offers a 2 in 6 chance of discovering the Maiden. She appears as a ghostly woman, young and pretty but with a face lacking even the hint of emotion. In a staccato voice, she will tell her visitors that she has been in this dreary place for many years, but soon will be returning home, though she won't give much more detail than that. Should the adventurers wish to leave, she will offer them a chance to defeat her at a game (the precise mechanics of this are up to the Referee, but a simple dice or card game should suffice). If the players win the game, the Maiden will rise and point her finger in the opposite direction. The adventurers, should they walk that way, will find themselves leaving the hex in a random direction (1 = North, 2 = Northeast, 3 = Southeast, 4 = South, 5 = Southwest, 6 = Northwest). If they fail, each person loses one level to the Maiden, who takes on a more lifelike appearance with each level she absorbs. The losers will have other chances to play the Maiden, either escaping with a success or losing another level with a failure. If they destroy the Maiden in a fight, they will find themselves no closer to escape and the Maiden will re-form after one week.

Maiden of the Maze: HD 4 (HP 20); AC 2 [17]; Atk 1 spectral touch (1d8 + lose 1 level); Move 15; Save 13; CL/XP 7/600; Special: Immune to non-magical weapons.

1614.

A village of jovial, diligent woodsmen rests here on a rolling meadow cut into the stifling forest. The woodsmen call their village Izabra, after an ancient empress of the Northmen. The village consists of 20 log cabins, partially dug into the earth, surrounded by a rampart studded with spiked logs and a moat of murky water. The men of the village have thick accents, owing to the fact that the men of the village are primarily Northmen, and the women of the village are from the winter tribes – mostly slaves taken by bandits. Thus, many of the villagers are of mixed ancestry, having light brown skin, dark red or black hair and blue to golden orange eyes. Coming as they do from two short races, they are themselves rather small in height, but stocky and muscular. The village is led by its priest, Lelmoth, who oversees a chapel of Lechta, the Northmen's moon goddess. The villagers employ an armorer known as Briggie to maintain their axes and spears and they maintain a long tavern decorated with wolf hides (some of them notably humanoid) that serves platters of roasted mushrooms and mugs of frothy ale. All 100 of the wiry villagers fight as well as men-at-arms, and one in ten carries a hand axe with a silver blade.

Lelmoth, Cleric Lvl 3: HP 13; AC 4 [15]; Save 13 (11 vs. paralysis & poison); CL/XP 4/120; Special: Spells (1st), turn

lycanthropes. Chainmail, shield, mace, holy symbol, sprig of wolvesbane tucked into a wide-brimmed, leather hat. Worships Lechta, a short, matronly moon goddess with a round, pleasant build and eyes full of moonlight (the eyes of her wooden idol are actual moonstones worth 35 gp each) and white skin. Lechta wears veils of moonlight and a silver tiara and carries a silver-bladed spear.

1702.

A crafty tribe of pixies, looking like gaunt little men with skin the color of fire and hair as black as soot, caper and play in this hex. The pixies, two dozen at least, are tricky and are equally likely to save a person's life as they are to endanger it. The pixies fear the Queen of the Winter Wind, and if one can get the better of them in test of practical jokes, they will reward the trickster with a firestone. The firestone looks like an oval stone about 8-inches in length and 6-inches in height. The stone, if set upon a pile of wood and tapped three times with a stick, ignites the wood and burns until tapped again, leaving the fuel unconsumed. The stone's greater power, however, is as a weapon. If the holder of the stone concentrates and squeezes the stone (this requires them to roll 1d20 under their Wisdom score), they can reduce the stone to about 2-inches in diameter. The stone will glow white hot, but it will not burn the holder's flesh. It can then be thrown as an 8 dice fireball. This use destroys the stone.

1705.

A column of 13 chanting, undead priests winds its way through the hills and dales, proclaiming the majesty of Death and its expansive country beyond the Black Water. The priests are garbed in a variety of vestments, indicating several different cults. The leader of the column holds a standard composed of half of a skeleton tied to a T-shaped pole, dozens of tarnished holy symbols (worth 300 gp total) clutched in its bony fingers. The priests hold rusty maces and flails. Their leader rides a pale horse. Two priests tow a cart filled with treasure, tribute to Death.

Treasure: 1,240 sp, 2,210 gp, funerary herbs worth 500 gp, and aquamarine worth 100 gp, two tiger's eye gems worth 175 gp each and four smilodon skins worth 30 gp each.

Undead High Priest: HD 4 (22 hp); AC 3 [16]; Atk 1 mace (1d6 + level drain); Move 9 (F24); Save 13; CL/XP 6/400; Special: Drain 1 level with hit, hit only by magic or silver weapons which inflict 1 point of damage per hit.

Undead Warhorse: HD 3 (12 hp); AC 7 [12]; Atk 1 bite (1d2), 2 hooves (1d3); Move 18; Save 15; CL/XP 3/60; Special: None.

Undead Priests: HD 3 (HP 15); AC 5 [14]; Atk 1 mace (1d6 + level drain); Move 9; Save 14; CL/XP 5/240; Special: Drain 1 level with hit, hit only by magic or silver weapons.

1711.

The unassailable redoubt of Dame Sciria, a chaste and zealous warrior-maiden of the Northmen, rests here at the fork of the river. A devotee of Valina, goddess of wildlife, she is an expert tracker and archer who commands a proud band of woodsmen armed with longbows and a love for their lady. Sciria has been engaged in a war against the humanoids north of the rivers for several years now, constructing her motte-and-bailey castle to aid in the struggle. Besides her 22 men-at-arms and 6 expert longbowmen (1st level fighters), Sciria has the assistance of Repric, a pale wizard from the south who joined her band after receiving visions. Although he has kept this a secret, he believes her to be the earthly incarnation of Eosinn, a hunting goddess of his people. He means to win her confidence and then steal her away, that he might levy a ransom on the gods for her return – hey, nobody said Repric was playing with a full deck.

Treasure: 1,750 sp, 2,920 gp, a jasper worth 35 gp and a *Manual* *of Beneficial Exercise.*

Sciria, Fighter Lvl 11: HP 58; AC 4 [15]; Save 4; CL/XP 11/1700. Chainmail, shield, light mace, longbow, 20 arrows, holy symbol of Valina. Sciria has an angelic face and a trim, athletic build. He is extremely intelligent and as well read as most magic-users.

Repric, Magic-User Lvl 4: HP 13; AC 9 [10]; Save 12 (10 vs. spells); CL/XP 5/240; Special: Spells (2nd). Tall, wide-brimmed black hat with a silver buckle and decorated with embroidered gold thread of celestial bodies (worth 50 gp), charcoal grey tunic and trousers, black cloak with a high collar and a gnarled staff of elder. Repric has pale skin, large, blue-grey eyes and a cruel mouth – made all the more cruel when he smiles, which is rarely.

1718.

This east bank of the Winding River is home to seven satyrs that arm themselves with shears and nets woven from human hair. They roam the area looking for victims to shear, humiliate and otherwise molest ignobly. Three of the satyrs carry pipes that can be used to cast charm person, sleep or fear. At night they are usually encountered chasing after pixies, sprites and nymphs, playing their cruel games. Encounters with the satyrs occur on a roll of 1-4 on 1d6.

Satyr: HD 5 (HP 20); AC 5 [14]; Atk 1 weapon (1d8); Move 18; Save 12; CL/XP 6/400; Special: 50% magic resistance, 90% concealment.

1724.

The hills here give way to a large meadow, the center of which is dominated by a massive dolmen. From afar, one can spy a figure in gleaming platemail sitting atop the dolmen, apparently in meditation. The meadow is littered with hundreds of bleached skeletons of animals and humanoids, all apparently intact. This is because the meadow is a massive colony of tangle weed. Folks walking out into the meadow will quickly find themselves attacked by the weeds and held fast. The tangle weed does not let up for a second, and in time the poor victim collapses and dies of thirst or hunger, or by strangulation if it gets a hold of their neck. The figure is itself a skeleton, the remains of a holy warrior who got to the dolmen but then found themselves too weak to escape the grass. The armor is adamantine platemail, with a base AC of 2 [17].

Tangle Weed: HD 4 (HP 20); AC 6 [13]; Atk 4 tendrils (1d6); Save 13; Move 0; CL/XP 6/400; Special: Entangle on roll of 1-2 on 1d6 and then automatic tendril damage each round from strangulation.

1817.

Obscured somewhat by a copse of large, black willows, there is a small, wooden boat landing. The landing juts about 20 feet into the river and is connected to a two-storey wooden tower that appears to have been abandoned for many years. The interior of the tower is damp and moldy, and contains a few scraps of furniture, a hearth thick with ashes and fish bones. A ladder leads to the second floor, with has narrow windows that look out over the river. A leather quiver holding five warped arrows rests next to one of these windows. A wardrobe on the second floor holds the grisly remains of a warrior, now in an advanced state of decay. People looking out of one of these second floor windows might notice dark shapes moving about in the water near the landing, and surely they will see the dozen water-logged zombies crawling from the water, their skin grayish-green, their eyes picked out by river fish. By this time, zombies coming from the forest will have surrounded the tower. Each zombie has a small cloth sack hanging from a leather necklace. The sacks hold a strange, powdery mixture and several teeth, which examination will suggest came from the zombie. Captives will be taken to the ruins in Hex 2216.

Zombie: HD 2 (HP 10); AC 8 [11]; Atk 1 strike (1d8); Move 6; Save 16; CL/XP 2/30; Special: Immune to sleep and charm.

1821.

In this hex one might come across the famed Golden House of Scarlad, an abbey of yellow limestone constructed atop a limestone ridge that runs parallel to the Great River from Hex 1624 to Hex 2018. This ridge is rich in copper deposits and contains a myriad of mines, tunnels and underground vaults dating from before the arrival of the northmen, but to which they have added considerably. The abbey can be approached from east or west via twisting, narrow trails that cut back often and are intersected by many small trails leading to old mines or good fishing spots, for the ridge harbors many fine fresh water ponds well regarded for their small, tasty, silvery fish.

Scarlad's Golden House is governed by Gwironod, a short, delicately featured man with piercing blue eyes and long hair that he keeps tied back. Gwironod is gracious, but argumentative on matters regarding religion, and fanatical in his desire to rid the region of goblins and other wicked humanoids. Despite his slight features, he is a whirlwind of violence when the spirit takes him and a competent warrior on horseback. His brothers number ten, all mounted religious knights who wear platemail lacquered with an aquamarine glaze in imitation of their god. They wield long maces and throwing hammers, and bard their warhorses in spiked platemail.

About one mile down the trail from the Golden House is the mining village of Frittany, the yellow limestone cottages of the miners being built above and within their copper mines. The village belongs to the abbey and is administered by a vicar, Folchon, assigned from among the holy brethren. Frittany houses about 70 miners and their families, along with a mad alchemist named Vassach (too much mercury exposure) and a penniless adventurer called Gaere of the Golden Eyes looking for some easy gold. The Harpy House, a tavern with a few subterranean rooms for rent, is the only place in the village a stranger can find a bed, food, drink and companionship. Visitors to the Harpy House should try the fish and berry stew or the roast boar's head, both specialties of the house.

Presently, Gwironod is seeking a golden key that was stolen from the abbey many years ago. The golden key activates the idol of Scarlad in the abbey's chapel, the idol being a lesser iron golem. He believes it is to be found in the possession of the strigoi in Hex 2018.

Treasure: 3,780 sp, 1,226 gp and twelve marten pelts worth 10 gp each.

Gwironod, Cleric Lvl 10: HP 44; AC 2 [17]; Save 6 (4 vs. paralysis & poison); CL/XP 12/2000; Special: Spells (5th), turn undead. Platemail, shield, warhorse in plate barding, mace, throwing hammer, holy symbol. Worships Scarlad, god of justice, who appears as a short, thin man with sapphire eyes, iron skin and wearing aquamarine armor.

Brother of the Golden House, Cleric Lvl 1: HD 1 (HP 5); AC 2 [17]; Save 15 (13 vs. paralysis and poison); CL/XP 1/15; Special: Turn undead. Platemail, shield, warhorse in plate barding, mace, throwing hammer, holy symbol.

Gaere of the Golden Eye, Fighter Lvl 4: HP 32; AC 4 [15]; Save 11; CL/XP 5/240; Special: Can cast charm person and read magic when out of armor. Dashing Northman rogue with golden eyes, threadbare clothing, well spoken, plays the harp and lute, claims to have been apprenticed to the archmage Tarucius of Fanch.

1913.

Nikkes, self-proclaimed Margravina of the Dales, looks defiantly north from the keep of her large, concentric castle. Styling herself "The Goddess-Fist", she is a devout worshipper of Vilmanna, goddess of vengeance and twin sister of Scarlad, the god of justice. Nikkes is a crusader, bent on clearing all the lands between the rivers of monsters and then constructing a line of forts to serve as the first line of defense for an expanded kingdom ruled by her guiding hand. Nikkes in aided in this quest by 15 valiant warrior maidens and 80 men-at-arms, all expert longbowmen. The precincts of her castle are crowded with peasants and herdsmen, attracted to Nikkes' might but not yet confident enough to live outside her walls. All of the gates and towers of Nikkes' castle are embossed with bas-reliefs of Vilmanna, who appears as a short, curvy woman with a bald head, aquamarine eyes and a forehead inscribed with a glyph of vengeance. The goddess wears rust-colored furs, carries a longbow and is accompanied by four wolves. Nikkes is presently low on funds, having just finished her stronghold a few months ago, and is thus looking for clever ways (e.g. tolls, taxes, fees) of rebuilding her fortune.

Treasure: 2,050 sp, 590 gp, seven fox pelts worth 14 gp each

Warrior Maiden, Fighter Lvl 2: HD 2+2 (HP 12); AC 2 [17]; Save 13; CL/XP 2/30. Platemail, shield, visored helm decorated with crimson streamers, battle axe, dagger, lance.

Nikkes, Fighter Lvl 9: HP 61; AC 2 [17]; Save 6; CL/XP 10/1400; Special: Enjoys the blessing of Vilmanna, allowing her to cast spells as a 3rd level cleric. Platemail, shield, visored helm decorated with crimson and yellow streamers, battle axe, dagger, lance.

2008.

A beacon tower of the Northmen, established to link the fortress in Hex 1906 and the village in Hex 2011, has been taken by goblins. Twenty of the scurrilous little dogs now occupy the place, armed with short bows and spears and commanded by a hobgoblin called Zugakh Longneck. The goblins are maintaining the beacon to give the impression that all is well.

Zugakh: HD 4 (18 hp); AC 4 [15]; Atk 1 weapon (1d10); Move 9; Save 13; CL/XP 4/120; Special: None.

2018.

Where a limestone ridge (see Hex 1821) turns back into the gentle, wooded hills common in this region, there stands the ruins of a large keep. The keep, constructed of crumbling yellow limestone blocks, once protected a caravan route between Yaryg and the Great River, but has since fallen into disuse. The keep was the possession of Lord Ullnus, a large Northman with a fiery temper and a brood of four equally unpleasant sons who made the mistake of attempting to shake down a strange visitor from "beyond". The visitor cursed the louts, turning them into strigoi (were-stirges), a form which they hold to this day. The priests of Scarlad in Hex 1821 have made a few forays against the strigoi, but have yet to destroy them. Father Gwirinod suspects that they possess the golden key he needs to animate his iron golem, and in this he is quite correct. It is held in an iron chest hidden beneath a paving stone somewhere on the ground floor of the keep along with 3,600 sp and 1,000 gp. The rafters of the keep are home to 12 stirges under the control of Lord Ullnus and his brood.

Strigoi: HD 5 (HP 30); AC 6 [13]; Atk 1 proboscis (1d4 + blood drain), 1 weapon (1d6); Move 12 (F12); Save 12; CL/XP 7/600; Special: Lycanthropy, drain blood (1d4), control stirges, only killed by silver weapons and fire.

Stirge: HD 1+1 (HP 6); AC 7 [12]; Atk 1 proboscis (1d3 + blood drain); Move 3 (F18); Save 17; CL/XP 1/15; Special: Blood drain (1d4), +2 to hit bonus.

2116.

The woods here are claimed by a troop of 15 mushroom men. The mushroom men are nomadic, moving about the woods looking for carrion, sometimes venturing into the grasslands at night to steal a carcass on which they can grow their young. The mushroom men have pale, slender bodies and large, hemispherical caps colored red-grey. They patrol their domain on the backs of giant man-sized centipedes and sometimes attack river traffic in dug-out canoes.

Mushroom-Man: HD 3 (HP 15); AC 5 [14]; Atk 1 spear (1d6); Move 12; Save 14; CL/XP 5/240; Special: Spores.

Giant Centipede: HD 2 (HP 10); AC 5 [14]; Atk 1 bite (1d8 + poison); Move 15; Save 16; CL/XP 4/120; Special: Poison (+6 save or die).

2202.

This hex holds an encampment of 100 Hivernians, mastodon hunters who travel south during the bitter winter freezes. The camp consists of dozens of leather teepees, all died black and held up by mammoth tusks (at least 1,000 gp worth in their present condition). The Hivernians are skilled hunters and fierce warriors, arming themselves with leather armor, leather-covered shields, war clubs and javelins that are hurled with atlatls (doubling their range). The Hivernians keep about 30 wolfhounds to aid in their hunting and guard the encampment when they are away.

Hivernian: HD 1+1 (HP 6); AC 7 [12]; Atk 1 weapon (1d6+1); Move 12; Save 17; CL/XP 2/30; Special: +2 to hit in berserker state.

Wolfhound: HD 2 (HP 10); AC 7 [12]; Atk 1 bite (1d6); Move 14; Save 16; CL/XP 2/30; Special: None.

2210.

Giant brain moles have dug maze-like burrows in the uneven prairie. The moles have white eyes can project a psychic blast once per turn. The blast has a conical shape, with a 20' length and a 10' base. Anyone caught in the blast must make a saving throw. Those who fail the saving throw must roll a d20. If the result is higher than their intelligence they suffer from a *feeblemind* effect. If the roll is under their intelligence, they are merely confused for 1d4 rounds. The long-legged goblins of the prairie have hidden cellars in the maze of burrows. Here, they keep prisoners, securing them with heavy masks and "mittens" of iron to keep them from wandering away.

To simulate the adventurers wandering in the burrows, roll on the chart below to describe the geography and check for random encounters. When a goblin cellar is discovered roll 1d6; a prisoner is present on a roll of 1, a treasure (100 gp) on a roll of 6.

Roll	Geography	Occurrence (1 in 6 chance per turn)
1	Passage slants down and to the right, 3d12'	Nothing
2	Passage slants up and to the right, 3d12'	Nothing
3	Passage slants down and to the right, 3d12'	Nothing
4	Passage slants up and to the right, 3d12'	Minor cave-in, save or lose 1d4 hit points and spend 1 turn digging out
5	Passage forks (roll 1d4 twice on this column)	Encounter 1d3 brain moles
6	Mole burrow containing 1d6 brain moles	Pass a concealed entrance to a goblin cellar

2214.

Orath is a village of thrifty woodsmen living in cozy stone cottages. Known for their large, intricate pipes (usually carved from bone or ivory), they chop down trees here and float them down river or take them by barge to Yaryg. Orath is surrounded by a wooden stockade and four watch towers. The Orathians are Northmen who love a good fight and never give in. Their elected leader, Mirssa, typifies the breed, and with her long, serpentine pipe and ever-ready axe, keeps man and beast in her neighborhood under control. The warriors of the village, 110 strong, are all skilled woodsmen and experts with the longbow and hand axe. Mirssa leads them personally, strapping on a long coat of bronze scales (treat as ring armor) and a shield decorated with a grimacing wolf chomping down on an armored arm when she wades into battle. The Orathians are not known for their hospitality, but they will allow strangers to bivouac outside their walls under the protection of their marksmen. Adventurers who keep a fire lit and post an additional guard are even paid 1 gp per night for their assistance in guarding the village.

Treasure: 180 gp.

Mirssa, Fighter Lvl 4: HP 22; AC 5 [14]; Save 11; CL/XP 4/120. Scale coat (ring armor), shield, battle axe, dagger, brass torc worth 6 gp.

2306.

The ruins of a stone keep and village smolder in this hex. A skilled guide should be able to identify the attackers as hobgoblins and, from the size of the holes in the walls of the keep, hill giants. The keep consists of the usual guard chambers, stables, great hall and lordly bed chambers, all burned and looted. The circular stairways in the corners of the keep have been trapped by the hobgoblins with trip wires that send barrels filled with stones down the stairs. Anyone on the stairs must pass a saving throw or suffer 1d6 points of damage. The only survivors of the hobgoblin assault are a family of pesky nixies living in the moat.

Nixies: HD 1d4; AC 7 [12]; Atk 1 weapon (1d6); Move 6 (S12); Save 18; CL/XP 1/15; Special: Charm.

2319.

A small tribe of gnolls occupy a wooded ridge at a point that allows them to make raids on several surrounding villages. The gnolls, numbering 60 warriors and twice as many females and young, make their living trading slaves to the terrible denizens of the Black Water. Their village is surrounded by a wooden stockade and divided into a high area for the chief, Yon, his 10 bodyguards (gnolls with 14 hp each) and harem of females, and a lower area for the common warriors. The slaves are kept in deep pits. The gnolls also keep a pack of ten hyenas that serve as guard animals. When encountered, there is a 1 in 6 chance that 25% of the warriors are off on raids led by 2 or 3 of the bodyguards and accompanied by 3 of the hyenas. If not away on raids, there is another 1 in 6 chance that half the tribe, bodyguards and hyenas are transporting a column of slaves to the coast.

Treasure: 2,210 gp in a terracotta coffer worth 10 gp.

Gnoll: HD 2 (HP 10); AC 5 [14]; Atk 1 bite (2d4) or weapon (1d10); Move 9; Save 16; CL/XP 2/30; Special: None.

Hyena: HD 1 (HP 5); AC 7 [12]; Atk 1 bite (1d3); Move 16; Save 17; CL/XP 1/15; Special: None.

Yon: HD 5 (20 hp); AC 4 [15]; Atk 1 bite (2d4+1) or weapon (1d10+1); Move 9; Save 12; CL/XP 5/240; Special: None. Equipped with a mail hauberk, tall shield and battle axe that can be thrown as a hand axe.

2416.

Yaryg is the last large settlement of the Northmen in the Winter Woods. A trading town, it is ringed by two earthen ramparts topped by wooden palisades patrolled by archers. Tall watch towers sport mangonels capable of launching showers of javelins on invading goblins. Yargyg is situated on a large, placid lake stocked with giant pike and fresh water bass. The lands around Yaryg are cultivated with grains, root vegetables, orchards of apple and cherry trees and hundreds of grazing goats. Most visitors to the town stay at Harper's Hope, a large coaching inn located between the inner and outer defenses of the town and famous for its goat and boysenberry

stew and steaming pike steaks. The town is ruled by Exfreza, once appointed Lord Governess by the Emperor of the Northmen, now self-styled Grand Duchess of the Winter Woods. Exfreza is a competent ruler, well liked by her soldiers and tolerated by her subjects. She is currently doing her best to solidify her position in the region and re-open caravan routes to the east, for stores of iron and steel and growing low since the region lost contact with the empire.

2503.

Three tall totem poles rise here from the grasslands. Each pole is about 25-ft tall and topped by a wooden carving of an animal spirit – wolf, elk and mammoth. The remainder of the pole is covered with geometric glyphs colored with reddish-black pigment. Climbing to the top of one of the poles and leaving a burnt offering to the gods has a 2 in 6 chance of attracting their attention. On a roll of 1 on 1d6, the supplicant has a 1st level cleric spell of their choice cast on them. On a roll of 6 on 1d6, the supplicant receives a snow owl as a spirit companion. The snow owl can communicate with the supplicant via telepathy and will be their boon companion for 1 week.

2514.

Carved into the bedrock here is a temple in the manner of the famous monolithic rock churches of Ethiopia. The temple is situated in a pit 60-ft wide and long and 30-ft deep. In the center of the pit and carved from the bedrock in a single piece, is the square temple, 30-ft tall and 40-ft wide and long. The temple has two stories and several chambers, all supported by stone pillars clad in dazzling aureate and scarlet tiles reminiscent of a serpent's scales. The interior is devoid of furnishings and the walls are coated with a contact poison that paralyzes in 1d6 rounds unless a saving throw is passed. A secret trapdoor in once chamber opens into a 30-ft vertical shaft with a long, bronze pole placed in its center to allow the serpent people who occupy the chambers beneath the temple to ascend and collect victims of their poison. Beneath the temple, the serpent people maintain a guard chamber, birthing chamber, great hall of science containing an alchemical laboratory and copper tablets engraved with eldritch secrets, a furnace kept hot by burning coal mined from beneath the hills, bedchambers and the chambers of their queen, Wyrmargilde. The serpent people of the Winter Woods are unique, for they are covered with downy, sable fur and possess red, horn-like protrusions above their eyes. While terribly wicked, they also possess a terrible hatred for the Queen of the Winter Winds, who drove them underground in ancient times. Should adventurers communicate to them their own desire to destroy the Queen, they might come to an understanding (e.g. not be made supper and sent on their way to kill the Queen). The serpent folk can offer adventurers a vial of reddish liquid they call the Blood of the Sun. It is poisonous to creatures of cold temperament like winter wolves, frost giants and the Queen, burning them from within, essentially killing them via spontaneous combustion. To other creatures, it grants immunity from cold for 1 day, but begins a month-long process of transformation into a furred serpent person.

Treasure: 2,490 gp kept in a brass coffer worth 1,000 gp.

Wyrmargilde: HD 6 (HP 30); AC 4 [15]; Atk 1 dagger (1d4) and bite (0 + poison); Move 12; Save 11; CL/XP 8/800; Special: Poison paralyzes for 1d6 turns unless a saving throw is passed, cast spells as 5th level magic-user and cleric.

Serpent Folk (20): HD 3 (HP 15); AC 4 [15]; Atk 1 two-handed axe (1d8+1) and bite (0 + poison); Move 12; Save 14; CL/XP 4/120; Special: Poison paralyzes for 1d6 turns unless a saving throw is passed.

2523.

In a thickly wooded valley crossed by dozens of narrow trails there rests a strange abbey. The building is a 6-story tower of grey brick topped by a copper roof. The ground floor of the abbey measure about 50-ft wide and long and contains a kitchen, storage rooms and dormitories ringed around an inner sanctum. The inner sanctum can be entered through one of four secret doors, each door set in the corner of a room and spinning on a central axis when one pulls a series of knobs in the proper order. Within the inner sanctum is the idol of Gevaloth, the God of Portals. Gevaloth's idol depicts a tall, broad chested man with black skin and sleepy grey eyes. Gevaloth wears archaic bronze armor and carries a wavy-bladed dagger in an upraised hand and a ring of keys in the other hand. The keys are actually chimes that, when struck in the proper order, cause a set of spiral, bronze stairs to erupt from a trapdoor in the floor in front of the idol to grant access to a concealed trapdoor in the ceiling. The inner sanctum is always kept warm by a dozen bronze braziers and guarded by four giant baboons on long chains that allow them access to the entire chamber, which measures 20-ft long and wide.

The spiral stairs in the inner sanctum lead up the second level and a hallway that rings the outer perimeter of each level. The hallway is a ramp, gradually moving people up to the very top of the tower. On the outer walls of the hallway are doors, one on each flat wall. These doors open into other dimensions, planes and locations on the Material Plane. As Referee, you should tailor the design of each door to the place it opens, so that clever players might guess what they're in for when they open a door. Doors might be locked and trapped, and strange creatures might be waiting on the other side when a door is opened. It is reasonable to assume that the higher one goes in the tower, the more bizarre the destinations of the different magic portals.

The abbey is overseen by Kadece, a regal woman in flowing black robes and a tall, conical gridelin hat from which she can conjure poisonous serpents that obey her commands. Kadece has 12 lesser priests in her order, all of whom take a vow of silence and wield wooden staffs carved in the likeness of intertwined serpents with steel heads shaped like screeching baboons. All wear chainmail beneath their robes.

Treasure: Kept in a locked iron coffer in the inner sanctum under the guard of the giant baboons. Consists of 5,950 sp, 266 gp, a wooden icon of Gevaloth worth 55 gp and a rolled up black bear pelt worth 15 gp.

Kadece, Cleric Lvl 9: HP 40; AC 5 [14]; Save 7 (5 vs. paralysis & poison); CL/XP 11/1700; Special: Spells (5th), turn undead, cast hold portal, knock and wizard lock 1/day.

Black Acolyte, Cleric Lvl 1: HD 1 (HP 5); AC 5 [14]; Save 15 (13 vs. paralysis & poison); CL/XP 1/15; Special: Turn undead, can cast hold portal 1/day and knock 1/day.

Giant Baboon: HD 3 (HP 15); AC 7 [12]; Atk 1 bite (1d8); Move 12; Save 14; CL/XP 3/60; Special: None.

2610.

The land drops into a boggy depression here, ringed by willows and crossed by a causeway of weathered stone. In the center of the hex there is a small upland topped by a village of Northmen who dredge iron deposits from the wetlands and trade it to the men of the south for farm produce. The village is composed of wooden cottages huddled around an abbey dedicated to Tazara, goddess of illumination. The abbey is composed of three 40-ft tall towers of alabaster topped by columns of light (created with round stones enchanted permanent light spells placed in basins of highly polished silver. These slim towers are connected by a triangular keep that holds a shrine of Tazara and living quarters for Maglara, the abbess, and her ten priests. The abbey holds an idol of Tazara, who appears as tiny, slender woman whose hair looks like rays of light. She has jade eyes and wears a lemon-yellow gown. On her arms are dozens of armbands inlaid with precious stones (can be stripped from the idol, worth 200 gp). In her outstretched hands she holds a cube of gold (worth 300 gp).

While the Abbey of Light was once a veritable beacon in the Winter Woods, it has fallen on dark times. Maglara and her priests have succumbed to the whispered promises of the Devourer, wicked spirit of winter. In a secret chamber behind the idol of Tazara they

have built a shrine to the Devourer where he receives sacrifices on moonless nights. The demon cult has spread through the village, with about 1 in 3 villagers now dedicated to the Devourer, having been promised protection when the Queen of the Winter Winds conquers the Winter Wood. Ten of the villagers now patrol the village at night in black, hooded cloaks and iron masks, kidnapping villagers to be brought into the cult or punishing those who oppose them. These "Iron Enforcers" and the priests all carry ritual daggers that look vaguely like icicles, being shaped more like spikes than blades.

Treasure: 520 sp, 1,700 gp, sardonyx dagger worth 9,000 gp and 20 barrels of mead (30 gal., 250 lb., 20 gp each).

Maglara, Cleric Lvl 10: HP 35; AC 4 [15]; Save 6 (4 vs. paralysis & poison); CL/XP 12/2000; Special: Rebuke undead, spells (5th). Chainmail, shield, mace, holy symbol. Rotund woman with ivory eyes, a round face and grey hair. She is judgmental and suspicious.

Acolyte of the Whispered Word (9), Cleric Lvl 1: HD 1 (HP 5); AC 4 [15]; Save 15 (13 vs. paralysis & poison); CL/XP 1/15; Special: Rebuke undead. Chainmail, shield, mace, holy symbol.

Priest of the Whispered Word (1), Cleric Lvl 3: HP 9; AC 4 [15]; Save 13 (11 vs. paralysis & poison); CL/XP 4/120; Special: Rebuke undead, spells (1st). Chainmail, shield, mace, holy symbol.

Iron Enforcers: HD 1 (HP 5); AC 7 [12]; Atk 1 dagger (1d4); Move 12; Save 17; CL/XP 2/30; Special: Surprise on 1-3 on 1d6, double damage during surprise round.

2618.

A village of rowdy, rough Northmen was built here to mine vein of rose quartz. The small village consists of a couple dozen hovels surrounded by a stone wall and moat of mucky rain water. The village is overseen by Mothionn, the younger half-brother of Exfreza, Grand Duchess of the Winter Wood, who lives in Yaryg in Hex 2416. The young baron, the title conferred upon him by his half-sister, commands a troupe of twenty men-at-arms in chainmail equipped with shields, axes and light crossbows. He lives in a small, round, stone tower in conditions only slightly better than the miners, sharing the tower with his soldiers and horses. He tolerates the conditions because he fears his half-sister and because the rose quartz mine is lucrative. Mothionn is using the money he skims from the operation to recruit assassins he plans to use to overthrow his sister after she has stabilized the region and brought it under her control. Currently, he has a swordswoman named Clevina in his employ. The miners live in a narrow valley, the sound of their singing echoing through much of the hex.

Treasure: 40 sp, 330 gp.

Mothionn, Fighter Lvl 3: HP 23; AC 2 [17] when armored; Save 12; CL/XP 3/60. Platemail, shield, battle axe, dagger, brass medallion bearing his family's arms (worth 25 gp).

Clevina, Fighter Lvl 6: HP 30; AC 6 [13] due to high dexterity; Save 9; CL/XP 7/600; Special: Surprise on 1-3 on 1d6. Leather armor, long sword, poisoned dagger (save or die), soft boots, three poisoned darts.

2704.

A meadow of honeysuckle and purple coneflowers stretches out as far as the eye can see. Tiny dragons with butterfly wings flit about, sampling the nectar and maybe discussing philosophy or the impending doom they sense from the west, and then taking off again. Encounters with 1d8 of the miniature dragons occur on a roll of 1-4 on 1d6. The beasts are content to ignore travelers, but are quite dangerous when riled.

Pixie Dragon: HD 1 (HP 5); AC 6 [13]; Atk 1 bite (1d2) and 2 claws (1d2) or breath weapon; Move 6 (F18); Save 17; CL/XP 2/30; Special: Breath weapon causes an allergic reaction (sneeze and cough for 1d4 rounds, no other actions possible) or sleep (as the spell), 10% chance of casting 1d3 level one magic-user spells.

2716.

Shirith is a village set on man-made terraces of limestone blocks on the steep banks overlooking the Swift River. The village has seven terraced levels, each ranging from 10 to 30 feet above the other and accessible only through tunnels and stairs that are blocked by iron portcullises. The villagers grow gardens of rare medicinal herbs in their misty river canyon, trading then to Yaryg for dried fish, grain, fruit and other essentials. The highest level of the village is a long reservoir fed by frequent rains. Irrigation pipes bring this water to the gardens. Shirith is ruled by the Baroness Sibevi, younger sister of the Grand Duchess of Yaryg in Hex 2416. Under her command is a corps of 60 crossbowmen in leather armor and wearing steel skullcaps decorated with pheasant feathers. The crossbowmen wield hand axes and light crossbows with poisoned bolts.

2725.

About 100 ill-tempered fishermen dwell in the center of this lake on a number of house boats that have been lashed together. The fishermen rarely venture ashore, afraid of the creatures of the nearby fungal moors. Each houseboat is a barge or raft topped by a simple hovel of sticks and equipped with a small iron stove and all the comforts of home (if your home is damp and fairly uncomfortable). Nobody rules the village, and strangers are unwelcome except in the direst of circumstances. One raft holds a small shrine to Uchai, the goddess of river otters. The shrine and the village are protected by four giant otters sent by Uchai in response to fervent prayer and sacrifice. Among the villagers there is a company of 10 rangers quite adept at slaying man and beast. The rangers are led by Black Ayla.

Treasure: 1,330 sp, 490 gp, soapstone idol of Uchai worth 45 gp.

Black Ayla, Fighter Lvl 6: HP 38; AC 5 [14]; Save 9; CL/XP 6/400; Special: 85% chance to track, +6 to hit and damage monsters. Ring armor, buckler shield, longbow, battle axe, dagger, orichalcum helm in the Roman style, worth 80 gp.

Rangers, Fighter Lvl 2: HD 2+2 (HP 12); AC 5 [14]; Save 13; CL/XP 2/30; Special: 65% chance to track, +2 to hit and damage monsters. Ring armor, buckler shield, longbow, battle axe, dagger.

Giant Otters: HD 3 (HP 15); AC 6 [13]; Atk 1 bit (1d8); Move 12 (S18); Save 14; CL/XP 3/60; Special: None.

2807.

In a high, narrow cave near the apex of a jagged shard of rock lives the manticore of the woods. Most folk in the region have heard of the beast, though few have ever encountered it and lived to tell the tale. It is indiscriminate in its predations, attacking humans and goblinoids alike. Many a column of gnoll slavers have lost their tribute to the Lords of the Deep to the manticore, and Saremunde in Hex 3108, has had many epic battles with the beast. The cave is quite inaccessible to folk without climbing equipment and experience or the ability to fly. Piled in the cave, which the beast keeps scrupulously clean, is a treasure of 890 sp, 1,480 gp and a pennywhistle. The pennywhistle is a powerful magic item, its shrill keening having the ability to control slugs, snails, worms, lampreys, leeches and other such creatures, and the ability to stun even the powerful aboleth (though all of the these beasts get a saving throw each round to ignore the whistle).

Manticore: HD 8+4 (53 hp); AC 4 [15]; Atk 2 claws (1d3), bite (1d8), 6 tail spikes (1d6); Move 12 (F18); Save 11; CL/XP 10/1400; Special: Flight, throw tail spikes up to 180 feet.

2910.

A great tangle of ley lines in this hex allows clerics and magic-users of any level to Control Weather over the entire map. The ley nexus takes the form of a stone table atop a barren hill, heavily weathered and marked with almost invisible lines that trace out the ley lines that run through the hex. All of these lines meet in the center of the table. A small cave in the base of the hill lives Toglo, an old shaman of the Hivernians, the guardian of the nexus. He allows none to step upon the table uncontested, and works for no side in the coming conflict between winter and spring. Toglo can summon one or two spirit creatures to aid him in his fight – a large unicorn representing the forces of spring and vitality, or a large hag representing the forces of winter and decay. Naturally, he will usually summon one or the other guardian, for in most cases the guardians would willingly aid natural allies of their season and oppose one another. To control weather from the nexus, a cleric or magic-user must stand atop the table and invoke powerful spirits of nature. To do this successfully, they must pass a saving throw, with magic-users suffering a -2 penalty to this roll. If the saving throw is made successfully, they can use the *control weather* spell and cover any portion of the Winter Woods map they wish. If they fail, they are struck with a bolt of lightning from the heavens, suffering 10d6 points of damage with no saving throw.

Toglo, Cleric Lvl 8: HP 43; AC 7 [12]; Save 8 (6 vs. paralysis & poison); CL/XP 10/1400; Special: Spells (5th), turn or rebuke undead, summon guardians. Leather armor (in the form of hides and furs), heavy mace, holy symbol.

Unicorn: HD 8+5 (HP 45); AC 0 [19]; Atk 2 hooves (1d10), horn (1d10); Move 24; Save 8; CL/XP 10/1400; Special: Double damage for charge, 25% magic resistance, teleport.

Hag: HD 10; AC 0 [19]; Atk 2 claws (2d8), bite (1d10); Move 12; Save 5; CL/XP 12/2000; Special: If hits with both claws the hag hugs and causes automatic claw and bite damage, polymorph self, summon mists.

3006.

On moonlit nights, thirteen wraiths that look like decrepit old Hivernians wearing wreaths of black roses around their necks and having iron nails in place of their teeth swarm from the ground to intercept travelers. The wraiths drain magic rather than levels. This magic drain can take the form of removing a "plus" from a magic weapon, a use from a magic staff or wand, ruining potions, scrolls and miscellaneous magic items, or stealing the highest level spell in a magic-user's mind.

Dweomer Wraith: HD 4 (HP 20); AC 3 [16]; Atk 1 touch (1d6 + magic drain); Move 9 (F24); Save 13; CL/XP 6/400; Special: Drain magic, only harmed by magic and silver weapons, which only inflict 1 point of damage to them.

3012.

A beautiful tower of polished marble rises from the hills here, set atop a granite promontory and approached by a narrow, winding staircase flanked by trellises of wild roses and lavender. Entry is gained through a door of bronze-colored wood equipped with a spy hole, the handle trapped by a minor ward of lightning (1d4 damage). The 30-ft diameter tower rises 50 feet and is topped by crenellations, through which grim hobgoblins with faces like rose-colored leather in tall helms of bronze and carrying light crossbows and curved swords. The tower is the home of Amaunter, a powerful magic-user, and his lady love Sifiet, a nymph. The two dwell in the heights of the tower in a room clad with marble rosettes and a pool of warm, clear water that issues from a fountain of gold cherubs. Amaunter and his lady rarely receive company, and one must have pressing business and a fine gift to see the wizard. The tower is guarded by 20 of the aforementioned hobgoblins as well as a troupe of 6 female pixies, Sifiet's handmaidens, and Amaunter's five apprentices, all drawn from the noble families of the town of Yaryg. Amaunter is a silver-tongued devil who falls easily for a pretty face (Charisma 15+). His

attentions on a female adventurer will result in terrible retribution by Sifiet and her goblins and pixies. Amaunter has entertained many such dalliances, usually in his private library, and has emerged unscathed from all of them.

Treasure: 4,920 sp, 4,340 gp, seven +1 sling bullets (made of silver, stamped with holy symbols), scroll of protection from dragons.

Amaunter, Magic-User Lvl 15: HP 30; AC 9 [10]; Save 7 (5 vs. spells); CL/XP 17/3500; Special: Spells (7th). Robes of bice embroidered with silver and gold thread, black staff, ritual wand composed of finger bones sealed with gold (worth 55 gp), silver dagger, brass waist chain set with turquoises worth 110 gp. Amaunter is a narcissist, loyal to none but himself.

Apprentices, Magic-User Lvl 1: HD 1d4; AC 9 [10]; Save 15 (13 vs. spells); CL/XP B/10; Special: Spells (1st). Bice robes, oversized berets, ritual wands of rosewood.

Sifiet: HD 3 (19 hp); AC 9 [10]; Atk none; Move 12; Save 14; CL/XP 5/240; Special: Sight causes blindness or death.

Pixie: HD 1 (HP 5); AC 5 [14]; Atk 1 dagger (1d4) or arrow; Move 6 (F15); Save 17; CL/XP 5/240; Special: Arrows, magic resistance 25%, spells.

3014.

A village of 70 dour human miners and 30 dwarves, dwell atop a vast salt mine in small, stone houses that are surrounded by a megalithic stone wall and a moat that also serves as a reservoir. The miners are ruled by a council of elders – three humans and three dwarves – and maintain a militia of 20 dwarves and men-at-arms. The salt mines and the stone wall are pre-human and date to the age of the serpent folk. Deep in the mine, the miners discovered an ancient statue of serpentine depicting a heavy, curvaceous woman with serpents for arms and legs. The statue sits cross-legged and in this position rises to 10-ft in height. In its lap is a large, alabaster egg. The eyes of the statue are made of multi-faceted crystal and are capable of hypnotizing (save or affected by powerful Suggestion) any who look on them. Over time, the discoverers brought the entire village under the idol's domination, killing those (mostly dwarves) who resisted. At night, the miners leave their village in large, armed parties to search for sacrificial victims. With each murder, a serpentine demon is forming in the alabaster egg – only three more need die to birth it into the world. If threatened, the idol will disgorge up to six iron cobras from its "hands".

Iron Cobra Mechanism: HD 3 (HP 15); AC 1 [18]; Atk 1 bit (1d4 + poison); Move 9; Save 11; CL/XP 5/240; Special: Poison (3 doses, save or die).

3017.

A tribe of 200 gnolls (plus 90 females and 330 cubs) has made its permanent camp in this hex atop a low ridge that has been cleared of timber, the timber being used to construct thick, tall walls and guard houses. The interior of this fortress is filled with filthy yurts and dozens of slave pits covered by wooden grates. A partially toppled beacon tower in the center of the village serves as the home of the chieftain, Wadawn and his harem of albino wise women. The gnolls, called "The Red Plague", have rust colored fur and use hide armor, hide-covered shields, spears and blowguns with poisoned darts (save or in 1d4 rounds become paralyzed for 1 round). The gnolls currently have 25 human slaves they are ready to drive to the coast. The gnolls are allied with two honking big trolls named Klev and Yorg.

Treasure: 1,000 cp, 770 sp, 1,370 gp in soiled fur sacks. The copper pieces are made of brass and almost look like gold pieces.

Wadawn: HD 4 (28 hp); AC 3 [16]; Atk 1 bite (2d4) or weapon

(1d10); Move 9; Save 13; CL/XP 4/120; Special: None.

Wise Women (5): HD 2 (HP 10); AC 6 [13]; Atk 1 bite (2d4) or weapon (1d8); Move 9; Save 16; CL/XP 3/60; Special: Cast spells and rebuke undead as 2nd level clerics, as a group they can cast one magic-user spell of 1st to 3rd level per day by chanting and dancing.

Gnoll: HD 2 (HP 10); AC 5 [14]; Atk 1 bite (2d4) or weapon (1d10); Move 9; Save 16; CL/XP 2/30; Special: None.

Hyena: HD 1 (HP 5); AC 7 [12]; Atk 1 bite (1d3); Move 16; Save 17; CL/XP 1/15; Special: None.

Klev & Yorg: HD 6+3 (33, 31 hp); AC 4 [15]; Atk 2 claws (1d4), bite (1d8); Move 12; Save 11; CL/XP 8/800; Special: Regenerate 3 hp/round.

3020.

A tribe of 60 sinuous, black lizardmen inhabits a series of half-submerged caverns in the shadow of the mushroom forest. The lizardmen are especially savage, disdaining the use of shields, weapons and fire. During the winter and autumn months they lie in a languid torpor in their slimy caverns, while in the spring and summer months they turn their rapacious appetites loose on the surrounding countryside. During the course of the year, they save the heads of their victims, preserving them with herbs and covering them with their waxy saliva. Each spring, they carry these heads, tied into bunches of three by their hair, to the shores of the Black Water and cast them into the sea as an offering to the Lords of the Deep.

Treasure: 3,560 sp, 120 gp.

Lizardman: HD 2+1 (HP 11); AC 5 [14]; Atk 2 claws (1d3), bite (1d6); Move 6 (S12); Save 16; CL/XP 2/30; Special: Breathe underwater.

3108.

Saremund, northernmost warlord of the Northmen and distant kin to King Polominen (see Hex 3222), is in the process of expanding his motte-and-bailey castle into a full-fledged concentric fortress – the so-called "tip of the spear" of Northman expansion into the Winter Woods. Unphased by reports of impending doom and unconcerned with the fall of the old empire (in fact, he does not believe a word of it), Saremund's boundless courage and optimism have drawn many Northmen to his banner – men and women looking to seize on a last glimmer of hope and glory. Saremund commands 20 men-at-arms, all skilled halberdiers in chainmail, and five knights of the old empire: Sir Amerior, Dame Brigis, Sir Fintoc, Sir Lespantio, Dame Sorra and Sir Valloc. All are battle-hardened veterans who intend to recreate their lost empire (for they know well that it has fallen) here in the Winter Woods. In this quest, they are assisted by Seghant, a crafty magician and exile of the old empire and a man Dame Sorra does not fully trust.

Saremund's home is always open to knights and their retinues, but others are not granted audience though they may be hired as mercenaries by Seghant, who acts as Saremund's vizier. The castle's grounds are inhabited by a small population at the moment – some herdsmen and crofters, but mostly masons, smiths and carpenters. Saremund is emptying his coffers constructing his castle and importing foodstuffs from the south, but he and his knights often supplement their stocks by hunting in the woods – there is a 1 in 6 chance that they will be encountered there, fully armored and carrying their normal complement of weapons plus longbows. These hunting parties are accompanied by ten men-at-arms as bearers, six hunting falcons and a pack of ten hunting dogs.

Treasure: 330 sp, 880 gp.

Lord Saremund, Fighter Lvl 10: HP 67; AC 1 [18]; Save 5; CL/XP 10/1400. Platemail +1, shield, lance, long sword, dagger, barded warhorse, silver brooch worth 1,550 gp, potion of clairvoyance. Saremund has piercing hazel eyes, coarse hair and a well-trimmed beard. He has a slight, though muscular build and always dresses in velvet and silk. He is irreligious and inquisitive and exudes confidence from every pore.

Sir Amerior, Fighter Lvl 7: HP 43; AC 2 [17]; Save 8; CL/XP 7/600. Platemail, shield, lance, battle axe, dagger, barded horse. Amerior is heavyset, with a long face that is always calm and commanding. He is a brilliant leader and men-at-arms under his command get a +1 bonus to hit and saving throws.

Dame Brigis, Fighter Lvl 5: HP 34; AC 2 [17]; Save 10; CL/XP 5/240; Special: +1 to hit and damage with bows when range is 30-ft or less. Platemail, shield, battle axe, dagger, longbow, barded warhorse, gauntlets of swimming and climbing. Brigis is among the younger of the knights. She has a round, pleasant face and figure and black eyes that seem to shimmer with starlight. She is romantic by nature and enjoys clever japes and jests.

Sir Fintoc, Fighter Lvl 6: HP 32; AC 2 [17]; Save 9; CL/XP 6/400; Special: Has a 1 in 6 chance of disarming opponents during each round of melee combat. Platemail, shield, lance, flail, dagger, barded warhorse. Fintoc is pudgy and serious, with a serious interest in courtly romance. He has a lovely young daughter named Clove who is the center of his universe.

Sir Lespantio, Fighter Lvl 8: HP 57; AC 3 [16]; Save 7; CL/XP 8/800; Special: Creatures hit by Lespantio must pass a saving throw or be knocked prone. Platemail, lance, heavy mace, dagger, barded warhorse, two armbands of black bronze worth 10 gp each. Lespantio is a bear of a man, with a craggy, bearded face. He is well traveled, speaks several dialects and has a melodramatic flair. He is a wonderful storyteller.

Dame Sorra, Cleric Lvl 7: HP 34; AC 2 [17]; Save 9 (7 vs. paralysis & poison); CL/XP 9/1100; Special: Spells (5th), turn undead. Platemail, shield, light mace, holy symbol. Sorra worships Scarlad, god of justice, above all others. A plain woman, she is tall, athletic, generous and chaste.

Sir Valloc, Fighter Lvl 5: HP 21; AC 2 [17]; Save 10; CL/XP 240; Special: +1 bonus to hit when wrestling. Platemail, shield, lance, battle axe, dagger. Valloc is young, impetuous and a bit stupid. He has deep, green eyes and a sweet nature, and thus is popular (though a bit clueless) among women.

Seghant, Magic-User Lvl 6: HP 17; AC 9 [10]; Save 10 (8 vs. spells); CL/XP 7/600; Special: Spells (3rd). Staff of crooked hickory topped with a piece of jet worth 115 gp, silver dagger. A tall man, bushy eyebrows and a heavily creased face. Disdainful manner before all but his lord.

3205.

A shadow mastiff lies dying, a pure white bolt in its side. If saved from death, it will be a boon companion to its savior.

Shadow Mastiff: HD 3 (16 hp normally, 0 currently); AC 6 [13]; Atk 1 bite (1d6+1); Move 18; Save 14; CL/XP 5/240; Special: Baying causes fear (flee for 3d6 turns), 40% invisible at night, in light movement reduced to 9 and loses 1d6 hit points.

3210.

Deep beneath the wooded hills, accessibly only through secret shafts that sink half a mile into the earth, is a funerary complex of the titans of old. Dedicated to the great and terrible Typhon, God-King of Monsters, the titanic halls and chambers of the complex were once used to inter the bodies of titans slain in battle with the gods. The crypts of these virtual demigods are protected by cunning magical traps and by such legendary monsters as the Minotaur, Sphinx and Chimera. The walls of the complex are covered in frescoes and mosaics depicting the titans interred beneath the earth and their master, Typhon, in battle with the gods. The floors are paved in porphyry and onyx, the 20-ft tall doors are cast of bronze and so heavy it takes a combined strength score of 40 just to budge them. Tomb robbers might encounter armies of bronze-clad skeleton warriors, iron golems, living, animated weapons, degenerate bat-winged harpies and fire-breathing hydras in addition to the aforementioned guardian beasts. The mind boggles at the thought of the wealth and magic to be found buried in the graveyard of the titans!

3222.

Here lies the "City of Madness". The city was once the primary colony of the Northmen in the Winter Woods region, the center of the northern expansion of their empire. They were unwise, however, to build so close to the Black Water and to attempt to wrest control of the moors from the ancient things that lived there. Prince Polominen, the founder of the colony, did not heed the advice of his advisors, and on the banks of the river he constructed a wondrous city of basalt towers with terraced gardens and alabaster plazas, divided by pleasant canals. As was predicted by his wise women and cunning men, the landscape soon conspired against him as though it were a living thing guided by a sinister intelligence. The spongy, black hills injected poison into the grain that was grown there; they loomed and seemed to grow, and the Black Water seeped into their canals and soon climbed over their banks. The great city now lies half-submerged in the oily water, its people driven insane and now taken to harvesting the fungal growths of the hills for their sustenance. The buildings host shrines of chaos, the bridges that connect them (for even the citizens of the City of Madness are not crazy enough to venture into the flooded canals) traversed by mad revelers who sell potent, narcotic wines, foaming priests who worship the Lords of the Deep, feral burghers who attack one another like animals, sparing not man, woman or child from their depredations, and shabby noblemen with keen, knowing eyes. And in the submerged palace, Prince Polominen, mummified in creeping black crud, still rules his great city and dreams of empire.

3303.

A large tribe of Hivernians, mastodon hunters, have made camp here. The camp consists of leather teepees surrounded by a spiked, wooden picket under the watchful eye of 20 expert archers (+1 to hit and damage with bows). The Hivernians spend their days hunting and the nights mending their equipment. One teepee in the center of the village holds a simple shrine to Yhoundeh – a small terracotta sculpture surmounted with elk antlers. A small emerald worth 300 gp is hidden inside the sculpture – it rattles around a bit. The chieftain, Jereran, is a bloody-minded individual who rules as much by fear as wisdom. His daughter, Llicha, is the village wise woman and an absolute terror with an axe. The tribe usually has 1d6 mammoth tusks, each worth 100-400 gp, in their possession.

Jereran: HD 5 (26 hp); AC 7 [12]; Atk 1 weapon (1d8 or 1d6); Move 12; Save 12; CL/XP 5/240; Special: Those under his command save vs. fear at +2 (since they're more afraid of Jereran). Leather (hide) armor, longbow, hand axe.

Llicha: HD 3 (12 hp); AC 7 [12]; Atk 1 weapon (1d6+1); Move 12; Save 14; CL/XP 4/120; Special: Can cast three 1st level cleric spells per day. Leather (hide) coat (beaded), longbow, hand axe, fetishes, ritual elk-head hood.

3421.

A tribe of 140 locathah dwell under the sea here in a sunken city. The city looks to have been designed for humans, or something very like humans. It has broad avenues paved in lapis lazuli, buildings with slanting walls that taper inward and domed roofs painted in complex arabesques done in brilliantly colored lacquers. The locathah go into battle mounted on giant eels and armed with tridents, nets and daggers. Their king is Aatharho, a large, broad-shouldered fish man who wears a crown consisting of a brass headband trailing a dozen thin, golden chains (worth 300 gp). The locathah worship the Lords of the Deep out of fear more than reverence, and resent giving them their maidens and young braves in tribute.

Treasure: 2,410 sp, 90 gp and a shagreen scroll with the spells detect magic, light, protection from evil.

Aatharto: HD 5 (27 hp); AC 5 [14]; Atk 1 weapon (1d8+1); Move 6 (S18); Save 12; CL/XP 5/240; Special: None.

Locathah: HD 2 (HP 10); AC 5 [14]; Atk 1 weapon (1d8); Move 6 (S18); Save 16; CL/XP 2/30; Special: None.

3510.

A large fortress rises here, protecting the entrance to a mine and founded by Gvart, a dwarven warlord who ignored advice from his clan and delved into the moors. The fortress and its mines are inhabited by 65 dwarves. All are covered in mottled, purple splotches and weird growths and have sleepy, drooping eyes with a look of madness in them. Gvart and his people dug into the land looking for gold, but instead found massive "truffles" of magenta streaked with grayish white. Unable to resist a strange compulsion to eat this fungus, they now subsist entirely upon it, and have dug an astounding number of tunnels and shafts in their desperate search for more of what they call "ambrosia". The ambrosia is slowly turning them into fungal creatures, and has infected them with paranoid delusions and a tendency to go berserk when challenged or aggravated. The dwarfs now pray to the Lords of the Deep, chaining captives on a tall, oily rock on the seashore at night as sacrifices to the aboleth. All of the dwarfs are capable of coughing spores when they fight. Assume that anyone in melee contact with a dwarf is surrounded by these spores, which attack the respiratory system, forcing those exposed to pass a saving throw or lose 1d4 hit points.

Lord Gvart, Dwarf Fighter Lvl 10: HP 48; AC 2 [17]; Save 5 (3 vs. magic); CL/XP 11/1700; Special: Notice stonework, cough spores, berserker (+2 damage). Platemail, shield, flail, hand axe. Craggier than the average dwarf, the fungal infection has begun to twist his legs, cutting his movement to 4. His black gums now support only three or four teeth, and his black tongue has become long and thick.

Fungal Dwarf: HD 2 (HP 10); AC 4 [15]; Atk 1 pick or axe (1d8+2) or 1 dart (1d4+2); Move 6; Save 16; CL/XP 3/60; Special: Cough spores, berserker. Chainmail, shield, pick or battle axe, darts (4).

3608.

There is what appears to be an ancient churchyard here holding a strange mausoleum. The mausoleum is built with phosphorescent green stone, with trapezoidal sides and a single trapezoidal door of black bronze bearing a knocker shaped like the head of a goat. The door can only be opened by using the knocker, which causes the door to silently vanish. Inside, the mausoleum is about 15-ft long and 10-ft wide, glowing softly and empty save for an open sarcophagus. Inside the sarcophagus are the skeletal remains of a tall man wearing a shimmering coat of mail (chainmail enchanted to never tarnish or rust) and holding a bronze goblet shaped like a skull. Water placed in the goblet and exposed to the sunrise turns into holy water. Water placed in the goblet and exposed to moonlight turns into a hallucinogenic poison (per the Confusion spell, duration of 1d3 days). Should one lay hands on the deceased, they will discover that the door has returned to its original position. It can only be re-vanished by placing at least 100 pounds of goods inside the sarcophagus (note that the goblet weighs 3 lb and the chainmail 50 lb, so if their weight must be accounted for if they have been removed.) Doing so causes

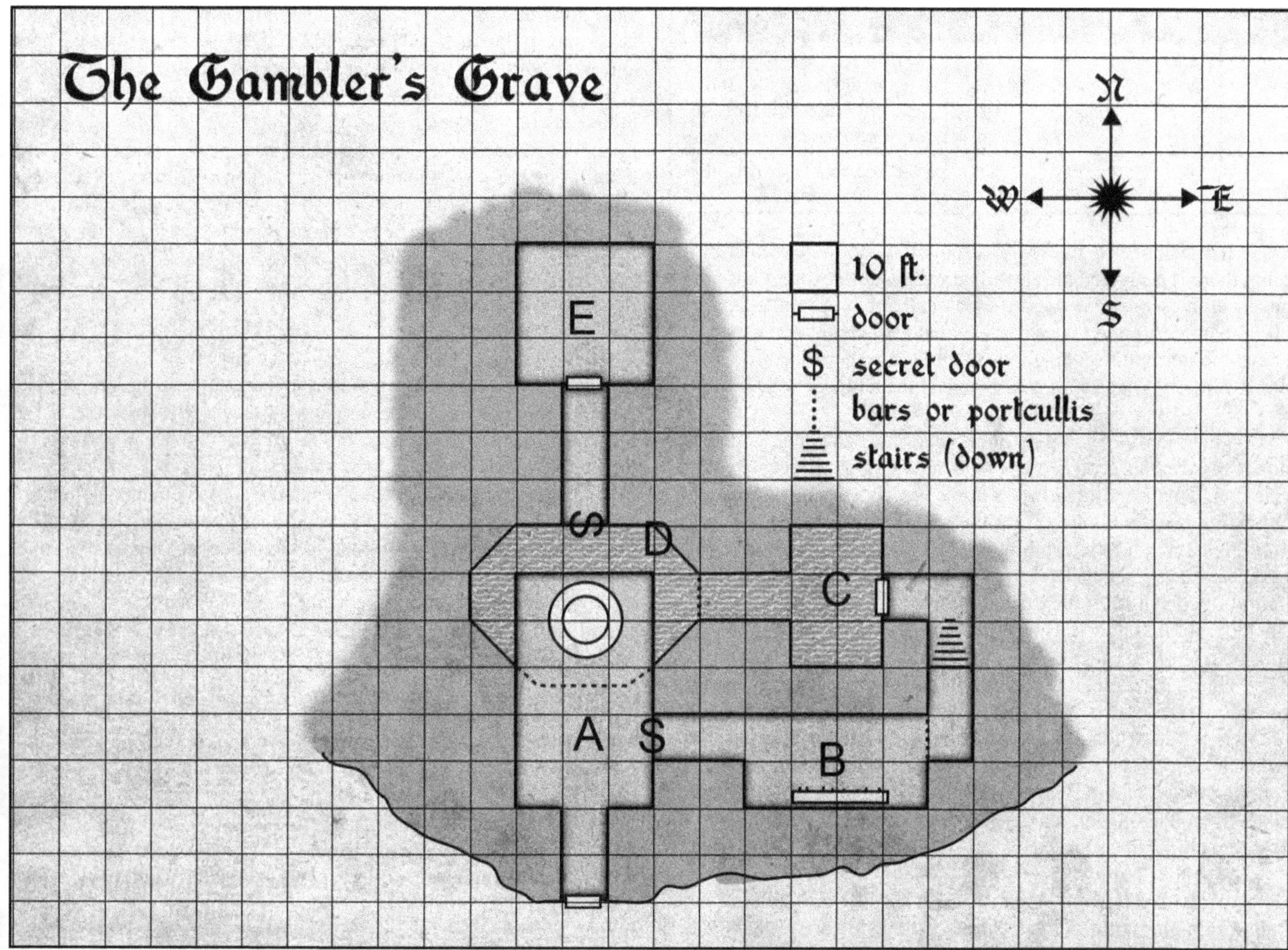

the door and the goods placed in the sarcophagus to vanish.

3624.

A tomb was excavated in this hex many years ago to house the remains of Lord Menry, an adventurer and early settler in the Winter Woods. The tomb is set in a limestone cliff, the entrance being a heavy bronze door set in a stone doorway. The location of the tomb is no secret, but nobody yet has discovered its secrets.

A – This long chamber has a low ceiling (5'). The chamber is carved directly from the limestone, and features a well decorated with bas-reliefs of dancing nymphs, and a bas-relief idol of Nephrut, the fickle god of fate and patron of gamblers. Nephrut looks like a short, plump elderly man with a bald pate dressed in a simple tunic (painted red, though the paint is well worn and chipped). The idol holds a thick book under one arm and has a knowing smile on his face. The well leads down to chamber D. The two secret doors can be opened by applying pressure with one's back or shoulder on the right-hand side of the door.

B – The floor of this chamber is paved with large, copper tiles, each about 5' x 5' and sounding hollow when tapped. Steel bars block the exit and a large, wooden wheel decorated with a number of disturbing images hangs on one wall. A bronze chain hangs from the ceiling, a clamp-like device on the end of it. By pulling the chain, two things happen. First, the clamp seizes the puller's hand and will not release until the chain has been pulled thrice. Second, the wheel spins, landing on a random space (see below).

Roll	Image	Effect
1	A man with a dagger over head	The iron bars raise, but will slam back down as soon as somebody passes under them. Make a saving throw or suffer 1d8 points of damage.
2	Lion swallowing a person	Random adventurer has a trapdoor open beneath him, plunging him into a pool of acid. Suffers 1d6 damage per round and cloth, leather and paper items are ruined.
3	Woman riding pegasus into sky	A random adventurer has electricity course through them from the copper tile beneath their feet, suffering 3d6 damage.
4	Headless man	A scything blade juts out from the north wall; all near the wall and not ducking (or halflings) must pass a saving throw or suffer 2d6 damage
5	A large eyeball	Adventurers hear a loud "clank", but nothing happens
6	Man torn in two by bears	Powerful magnets are activated in the north and south walls; characters in metal armor must roll under their strength score on 2d12 or suffer 1d8 points of damage.

Roll	Image	Effect
7	Mermaid kissing a drowning man	Poison gas spews into the room; disipates after 1d6 rounds; causes blindness in those who fail a saving throw
8	Grinning death	The iron bars raise, but close 10 minutes later

C – This chamber is filled with a foot of water. In the center of the room there is a covered pit, also filled with water. As one steps on the cover, it gives way, but quickly snaps shut again. A total strength of 20 is required to open the cover. The pit also contains a winch that opens the portcullis leading into room D. The corridor to D slopes downward, the water being waist-high at the entrance to D.

D – This room is filled waist-high with brackish water, and slopes down toward the center. A grey ooze dwells in the center of the chamber. The secret door in the north wall is only large enough to crawl through and is located near the ceiling. The passage to E is also only high enough to crawl through, and is trapped midway through by a pressure plate that releases dozens of metal spikes from the floor, inflicting 1d8 damage (save for half) on all inside the passage. The door into room E is a metal grate.

E – This is the tomb of Menry, a hoary old corpse in dusty, crimson funerary robes and a broad-brimmed hat with a phoenix feather (confers 50% resistance to fire) stuck in the band. The corpse sits at a wooden table, a stack of cards under one bony hand and three cards face up in front of him. Three coffers sit behind him, one copper, one silver and one gold (foil only – worth about 5 gp, 50 gp and 500 gp respectively). All are locked.

The cards depict a red knight triumphant over a dragon, a white knight climbing golden hair hanging from a tower window, and a yellow knight standing in a pot of boiling water.

The copper chest holds a dessicated corpse that springs out of the coffer and attacks as mummy (34 hp). The gold coffer releases a small fire elemental (37 hp). The silver coffer holds a rope woven from golden hair that immediately animates and attempts to strangle whoever holds it. Treat it as a 4 HD creature with 20 hp and immune to bludgeoning attacks. On a successful attack, it winds around its victim's neck and causes 1d6 damage per round thereafter until destroyed or pried loose. The real treasure in the room is the deck of cards, which confer a +2 bonus to saving throws for the person who holds them. The cards can also divine one danger per day – the holder draws a card and, if there is a danger within 20 feet, the card depicts it in a whimsical image like those displayed on the table.

3705.

This hex is patrolled at night by mutated humanoids with translucent skin that shows off their bright, purple veins. These strange, miserable folk hate light and fear fire and while they can breathe water and air, they give off a gurgling wheeze when they do so. They hunt the land for victims to bring down into the water for their fishy masters. The kiss of these mutants gives humans the ability to breathe water for up to 3 hours – long enough to reach the submarine temples of the Lords of the Deep.

Mutant: HD 2 (HP 10); AC 6 [13]; Atk 1 strike (1d8) or silver net (as hold person spell); Move 12 (S12); Save 16; CL/XP 2/30; Special: Breathe water.

4010.

In vaguely the center of the hex, there is a column of airy water that extends from the surface of the water to the sea floor. Airy water is, for all intents and purposes, water that air-breathing and water-breathing creatures can breathe normally. In all other ways, it behaves as water. This particular column is approximately 100-ft in diameter

and allows access to an undersea diamond mine. The mine's entrance is a small pillar of basalt that rises about 15-ft from the sea floor and is roughly 7-ft in diameter. A copper grate in the pillar allows access to the mine, which was excavated by an unknown agent many thousands of years ago. Most of the mine is filled with airy water, though there are some deadfalls filled with heavy, black water, and many traps spew poisons into the airy water to kill the unwary. The mine is heated by volcanic action in the lower levels, and inhabited by a multitude of strange beings, including renegade locathah, a band of monster-slaying mermaids, aquatic oozes, gigantic sucker fish and mutated humans like the ones that appear in Hex 3705.

4023.

A small statue carved from marble and depicting a cherubic human male in a tunic stands here on an open meadow. The statue is 3-ft tall and missing a foot. It points to the east, toward the shores of the Black Water where, in fact, its missing foot has been deposited in the muck and grime (normal folk have a 1 in 6 chance per day of finding it if they follow the pointing finger to the shore, elves a 2 in 6 chance). If the foot is returned to the statue and put in its proper place, the statue turns into a pallid, gnomish creature that presents its benefactor with a nugget of gold and the scurries off into the woodlands. The nugget is actually a gold dragon egg that, if kept warm, will hatch in 1d4+4 weeks.

What Does the Rise of the Queen of the Winter Wind Mean?

The gradual glaciation of a region does not make for high adventure, but such a situation can be turned into such by thinking allegorically. Much of the folklore and mythology we all enjoy is allegorical and symbolic in nature. So, perhaps the rise of the Queen brings an invasion of the Winter Woods by an army of frost giants, polar bear-mounted bugbears, winter wolves and pixies that fire enchanted icicles from their bows. As this strange army moves south, the rivers freeze, glaciers push through the canyons and valleys, and an ice sheet grows over the landscape, killing just about everything in its path. To stop the advance of ice, one must battle the invading army – defeating the frost giants becomes a symbolic victory of spring over winter. Or perhaps the Queen brings a spiritual winter with her – the skies turn grey and black, winter never ends, nothing grows, and people become cold and heartless toward one another. With little food and former allies turned into enemies, the adventurers must push into the north and defeat the Queen, the source of this spiritual and physical malaise.

New Monsters

Aboleth

Aboleths are orca-sized creatures resembling sleek, slimy catfish with lashing tentacles in place of whiskers and multiple, eyes placed on their heads. Aboleths are terribly ancient and evil. They are amphibious and might be found at the bottom of dark lakes or seas or dwelling underground. They can cast charm monster three times per day and phantasmal force three times per day. Aboleths are surrounded by clouds of mucus that re quire anyone inhaling it to make a saving throw or become a water-breather (and not an air-breather) for 3 hours. The slime on the creature's tentacles causes a disease unless a saving throw is made. The disease causes one's skin to change, becoming translucent and requiring the afflicted to be immersed in water once per hour or suffer 1d6 points of damage.

Aboleth: HD 9 (HP 45); AC 3 [16]; Atk 4 tentacles (1d6 + slime); Save 6; Move 9 (S12); CL/XP 12/2000; Special: Charm monster 3/day, phantasmal force 3/day, mucus cloud, tentacle slime disease.

Ankheg

Ankhegs are large insects resembling locusts that bore through the ground, often coming under their prey and snatching them down into their tunnels before they know what hit them. Once per day they can squirt digestive acids for 5d6 points of damage (save for half) as a defensive tactic.

Ankheg: HD 5 (HP 10); AC 2[17]; Atk 1 bite (3d6); Move 12 (B6); Save 12; CL/XP 6/400; Special: Spits acid.

Giant Animal

Giant animals look and behave like their normal-sized kin, but are generally two or three times as large.

Giant Alligator: HD 6 (HP 30); AC 3 [16]; Atk 1 bite (3d6), tail (1d6); Move 9 (S12); Save 11; CL/XP 6/400; Special: None.

Giant Badger: HD 3 (HP 15); AC 4 [15]; Atk 2 claws (1d3), bite (1d6); Move 6; Save 14; CL/XP 3/60; Special: None.

Giant Eagle: HD 4 (HP 20); AC 7 [12]; Atk 2 talons (1d4), bite (1d8); Move 3 (F24); Save 13; CL/XP 4/120; Special: None.

Giant Frog: HD 3 (HP 15); AC 7 [12]; Atk 1 bite (1d8); Move 3 (or 100' leap); Save 14; CL/XP 4/120; Special: Leap, swallow whole on a natural attack roll of '20', victim dies in 3 rounds unless cuts self out with an attack roll of '18' or higher, which also slays the frog.

Giant Skunk: HD 4 (HP 20); AC 7 [12]; Atk 1 bite (1d6); Move 9; Save 13; CL/XP 6/400; Special: Sprays musk (dissolves paper and cloth 100%, leather 20%, causes nausea for 1d6 turns (saving throw) and blindness for 3d6 turns (saving throw), stench remains forever until 1d6 days of washing are completed).

Locathah

Locathah are primitive humanoids that are more fish than man. Their bodies are covered in fish scales and their heads have large fish eyes and gaping mouths filled with needle-like teeth. Locathah use shields, tridents, spears, crossbows and nets in combat and often share their homes with giant eels and crabs, which they use as mounts, guard animals and beasts of burden.

Locathah: HD 2 (HP 10); AC 5 [14]; Atk 1 weapon (1d8); Move 6 (S18); Save 16; CL/XP 2/30; Special: None.

Mastodon

Mastodons are enormous elephants with large tusks.

Mastodon: HD 12 (HP 60); AC 5 [14]; Atk 1 trunk (1d10), 2 tusks (1d10+4), 2 stomps (2d6+4); Move 12; Save 3; CL/XP 13/2300; Special: None.

Mushroom Man

Mushroom men look like walking, humanoid mushrooms, with beady black eye buds and slit mouths beneath their mushroom caps and thick, stunted arms and legs springing from their mushroom stalk bodies. They are simple folk, employing clubs and spears as weapons. When a mushroom man dies it releases 1d6 spores which rapidly (within 1d4 rounds) develop into mushroom men of 1 HD lower than their parent. 1 HD mushroom men do not produce spores. Spores have 2 hp before they become fully formed mushroom men.

Mushroom-Man: HD 3 (HP 15); AC 5 [14]; Atk 1 spear (1d6); Move 12; Save 14; CL/XP 5/240; Special: Spores.

Smilodon

Smilodons are large felines that resemble tawny-furred tigers with large, sabre-like teeth. If they hit with both of their fore claws, they gain 2 additional attacks with their rear claws.

Smilodon: HD 7 (HP 35); AC 6 [13]; Atk 2 claws (1d4+1), bite (2d6); Move 12 (S6); Save 10; CL/XP 8/800; Special: Rear claws.

Violet Fungi

Violet fungi are large, purple mushrooms with tentacles (2 to 3 feet long) growing from the base. These tentacles allow the mushrooms to move slowly. A hit from a tentacle causes flesh to rot (saving throw applies) unless a cure disease spell is cast on the afflicted area.

Violet Fungi: HD 3 (HP 15); AC 7 [12]; Atk 4 tendrils (rot); Move 1; Save 14; CL/XP 4/120; Special: Rot.

Wendigo

A wendigo is, essentially, a living ghoul. They are humanoids who have become lost in the wilderness and turned to cannibalism to survive. As wendigos, they exist in a feral state, retaining some portion of their intelligence, but behaving more like cunning animals.

Wendigo: HD 4 (HP 20); AC 4 [15]; Atk 1 bite (1d6); Move 15; Save 13; CL/XP 4/120; Special: Immune to cold, only killed by silver or magic weapons – otherwise regenerate 2 hp per turn after "death".

Winter Wolf

Winter wolves are massive, intelligent wolves with white fur. Winter wolves can breathe a cone of frost, blasting everything in front of them within 10 feet for 4d6 points of damage (save for half). This ability can only be used once every 10 rounds.

Winter Wolf: HD 5 (HP 25); AC 5 [14]; Atk 1 bite (1d6+1); Move 18; Save 12; CL/XP 6/400; Special: Breathe frost.

OGL Notes

The following monsters were taken from the S&W Monster Book 0E Core Rules – Aboleth, Mushroom Man, Giant Badger, Giant Eagle, Giant Skunk, Giant Frog, Violet Fungi, Sabre-tooth tiger (smilodon), Winter Wolf, Mammoth (mastodon).

Hex Crawl Chronicles: The Winter Woods is written under version 1.0a of the Open Game License. As of yet, none of the material first appearing in **Hex Crawl Chronicles: The Winter Woods** is considered Open Game Content.

OPEN GAME LICENSE Version 1.0a

The following text is the property of Wizards of the Coast, Inc. and is Copyright 2000 Wizards of the Coast, Inc ("Wizards"). All Rights Reserved.

1. Definitions: (a)"Contributors" means the copyright and/or trademark owners who have contributed Open Game Content; (b)"Derivative Material" means copyrighted material including derivative works and translations (including into other computer languages), potation, modification, correction, addition, extension, upgrade, improvement, compilation, abridgment or other form in which an existing work may be recast, transformed or adapted; (c) "Distribute" means to reproduce, license, rent, lease, sell, broadcast, publicly display, transmit or otherwise distribute; (d)"Open Game Content" means the game mechanic and includes the methods, procedures, processes and routines to the extent such content does not embody the Product Identity and is an enhancement over the prior art and any additional content clearly identified as Open Game Content by the Contributor, and means any work covered by this License, including translations and derivative works under copyright law, but specifically excludes Product Identity. (e) "Product Identity" means product and product line names, logos and identifying marks including trade dress; artifacts; creatures characters; stories, storylines, plots, thematic elements, dialogue, incidents, language, artwork, symbols, designs, depictions, likenesses, formats, poses, concepts, themes and graphic, photographic and other visual or audio representations; names and descriptions of characters, spells, enchantments, personalities, teams, personas, likenesses and special abilities; places, locations, environments, creatures, equipment, magical or supernatural abilities or effects, logos, symbols, or graphic designs; and any other trademark or registered trademark clearly identified as Product identity by the owner of the Product Identity, and which specifically excludes the Open Game Content; (f) "Trademark" means the logos, names, mark, sign, motto, designs that are used by a Contributor to identify itself or its products or the associated products contributed to the Open Game License by the Contributor (g) "Use", "Used" or "Using" means to use, Distribute, copy, edit, format, modify, translate and otherwise create Derivative Material of Open Game Content. (h) "You" or "Your" means the licensee in terms of this agreement.

2. The License: This License applies to any Open Game Content that contains a notice indicating that the Open Game Content may only be Used under and in terms of this License. You must affix such a notice to any Open Game Content that you Use. No terms may be added to or subtracted from this License except as described by the License itself. No other terms or conditions may be applied to any Open Game Content distributed using this License.

3.Offer and Acceptance: By Using the Open Game Content You indicate Your acceptance of the terms of this License.

4. Grant and Consideration: In consideration for agreeing to use this License, the Contributors grant You a perpetual, worldwide, royalty-free, non-exclusive license with the exact terms of this License to Use, the Open Game Content.

5.Representation of Authority to Contribute: If You are contributing original material as Open Game Content, You represent that Your Contributions are Your original creation and/or You have sufficient rights to grant the rights conveyed by this License.

6.Notice of License Copyright: You must update the COPYRIGHT NOTICE portion of this License to include the exact text of the COPYRIGHT NOTICE of any Open Game Content You are copying, modifying or distributing, and You must add the title, the copyright date, and the copyright holder's name to the COPYRIGHT NOTICE of any original Open Game Content you Distribute.

7. Use of Product Identity: You agree not to Use any Product Identity, including as an indication as to compatibility, except as expressly licensed in another, independent Agreement with the owner of each element of that Product Identity. You agree not to indicate compatibility or co-adaptability with any Trademark or Registered Trademark in conjunction with a work containing Open Game Content except as expressly licensed in another, independent Agreement with the owner of such Trademark or Registered Trademark. The use of any Product Identity in Open Game Content does not constitute a challenge to the ownership of that Product Identity. The owner of any Product Identity used in Open Game Content shall retain all rights, title and interest in and to that Product Identity.

8. Identification: If you distribute Open Game Content You must clearly indicate which portions of the work that you are distributing are Open Game Content.

9. Updating the License: Wizards or its designated Agents may publish updated versions of this License. You may use any authorized version of this License to copy, modify and distribute any Open Game Content originally distributed under any version of this License.

10. Copy of this License: You MUST include a copy of this License with every copy of the Open Game Content You Distribute.

11. Use of Contributor Credits: You may not market or advertise the Open Game Content using the name of any Contributor unless You have written permission from the Contributor to do so.

12. Inability to Comply: If it is impossible for You to comply with any of the terms of this License with respect to some or all of the Open Game Content due to statute, judicial order, or governmental regulation then You may not Use any Open Game Material so affected.

13. Termination: This License will terminate automatically if You fail to comply with all terms herein and fail to cure such breach within 30 days of becoming aware of the breach. All sublicenses shall survive the termination of this License.

14. Reformation: If any provision of this License is held to be unenforceable, such provision shall be reformed only to the extent necessary to make it enforceable.

15. COPYRIGHT NOTICE

Open Game License v 1.0a Copyright 2000, Wizards of the Coast, Inc.

System Reference Document Copyright 2000-2003, Wizards of the Coast, Inc.; Authors Jonathan Tweet, Monte Cook, Skip Williams, Rich Baker, Andy Collins, David Noonan, Rich Redman, Bruce R. Cordell, John D. Rateliff, Thomas Reid, James Wyatt, based on original material by E. Gary Gygax and Dave Arneson.

Swords & Wizardry Core Rules, Copyright 2008, Matthew J. Finch
Monster Compendium: 0e, Copyright 2008, Matthew J. Finch

www.ingramcontent.com/pod-product-compliance
Lightning Source LLC
Chambersburg PA
CBHW081329090726
47907CB00010B/2425